WRESTLING MATCH

Clint had managed to turn halfway around before he felt Abe's arms wrap around his midsection. Those arms closed in a painful bear hug that lifted Clint completely off his feet. He was trapped at such an odd angle that it took him a moment to get his bearings. When he did, he realized just how much trouble he was in.

"Shoot this bastard, Matt," Abe grunted.

The moment Abe had spoken those words, Clint managed to slam a heel into Abe's knee. That was enough for Clint to get his own feet back on the ground again, but not quite enough to loosen Abe's hold. The man was still drunk as a skunk and had the strength of a lunatic to go along with it. Rather than try to bargain any longer, Clint swung around to face Abe while lashing out with a right hook.

Clint's punch had more momentum than a steam engine racing downhill. When his fist connected with Abe's face, he nearly took the drunk's head off his shoulders. The impact made a dull cracking sound and sent a spray of bloody spit through the air . . .

DON'T MISS THESE
ALL-ACTION WESTERN SERIES
FROM THE BERKLEY PUBLISHING GROUP

THE GUNSMITH by J. R. Roberts
Clint Adams was a legend among lawmen, outlaws, and ladies. They called him . . . the Gunsmith.

LONGARM by Tabor Evans
The popular long-running series about Deputy U.S. Marshal Long—his life, his loves, his fight for justice.

SLOCUM by Jake Logan
Today's longest-running action Western. John Slocum rides a deadly trail of hot blood and cold steel.

BUSHWHACKERS by B. J. Lanagan
An action-packed series by the creators of Longarm! The rousing adventures of the most brutal gang of cutthroats ever assembled—Quantrill's Raiders.

DIAMONDBACK by Guy Brewer
Dex Yancey is Diamondback, a Southern gentleman turned con man when his brother cheats him out of the family fortune. Ladies love him. Gamblers hate him. But nobody pulls one over on Dex . . .

WILDGUN by Jack Hanson
The blazing adventures of mountain man Will Barlow—from the creators of Longarm!

TEXAS TRACKER by Tom Calhoun
Meet J.T. Law: the most relentless—and dangerous—manhunter in all Texas. Where sheriffs and posses fail, he's the best man to bring in the most vicious outlaws—for a price.

THE GUNSMITH

294

FAREWELL MOUNTAIN

J. R. ROBERTS

JOVE BOOKS, NEW YORK

THE BERKLEY PUBLISHING GROUP
Published by the Penguin Group
Penguin Group (USA) Inc.
375 Hudson Street, New York, New York 10014, USA
Penguin Group (Canada), 90 Eglinton Avenue East, Suite 700, Toronto, Ontario M4P 2Y3, Canada
(a division of Pearson Penguin Canada Inc.)
Penguin Books Ltd., 80 Strand, London WC2R 0RL, England
Penguin Group Ireland, 25 St. Stephen's Green, Dublin 2, Ireland (a division of Penguin Books Ltd.)
Penguin Group (Australia), 250 Camberwell Road, Camberwell, Victoria 3124, Australia
(a division of Pearson Australia Group Pty. Ltd.)
Penguin Books India Pvt. Ltd., 11 Community Centre, Panchsheel Park, New Delhi—110 017, India
Penguin Group (NZ), Cnr. Airborne and Rosedale Roads, Albany, Auckland 1310, New Zealand
(a division of Pearson New Zealand Ltd.)
Penguin Books (South Africa) (Pty.) Ltd., 24 Sturdee Avenue, Rosebank, Johannesburg 2196,
South Africa

Penguin Books Ltd., Registered Offices: 80 Strand, London WC2R 0RL, England

This is a work of fiction. Names, characters, places, and incidents either are the product of the author's imagination or are used fictitiously, and any resemblance to actual persons, living or dead, business establishments, events, or locales is entirely coincidental.

FAREWELL MOUNTAIN

A Jove Book / published by arrangement with the author

PRINTING HISTORY
Jove edition / June 2006

Copyright © 2006 by Robert J. Randisi.

ISBN: 0-515-14145-3

JOVE®
Jove Books are published by The Berkley Publishing Group,
a division of Penguin Group (USA) Inc.,
375 Hudson Street, New York, New York 10014.
JOVE is a registered trademark of Penguin Group (USA) Inc.
The "J" design is a trademark belonging to Penguin Group (USA) Inc.

PRINTED IN THE UNITED STATES OF AMERICA

10 9 8 7 6 5 4 3 2 1

ONE

It was a cloudy day in a little town called Mud Foot. Despite the name, it actually wasn't a bad town. Situated deep in Montana Territory, Mud Foot was built on a river of the same name and was in sight of a beautiful stretch of mountains that had broken the backs of more than its share of miners.

Clint had found his way there a few days ago when he was in dire need of supplies. As of yet, he was still inclined to stay on for a bit. Mud Foot was one of those places that felt like its own little world. Being nestled in the mountains tended to do that to towns and men alike, making both feel like their own little islands away from the mainland.

Of course, the Georgia Peach Saloon had a little something to do with Clint's decision as well. The rooms there were clean and cheap. The food they served was tasty and the card tables were always busy. At the moment, Clint was mostly concerned with the latter and had been for the better part of a day.

Clint sat at a small round table with three others. The man to his left was a miner in his thirties named Abe. Abe was a big fellow with the build of someone who was accustomed to making his living by moving heavy things. His

1

hands were rough and he had the mannerisms of someone more used to dealing with rocks, shovels, and logs than people.

Abe didn't talk much and when he did, there was usually a good amount of profanity tossed in. He didn't drink much either, and wasn't too good at cards. Since he'd just cashed in a few pouches of gold dust, however, nobody at the table had a problem with him.

Sitting to Abe's left was a man in his mid-twenties named Melvin Grimley. Although Melvin talked more than enough to pick up Abe's slack, he didn't actually say much. Most of what came out of his mouth was bluster and the rest was gossip. The only real difference between the two was if his words were about himself or someone else.

Melvin had skin that had been baked to a dark brown after years spent under the sun. His hair was a thick black mat on top of his head that hung down almost long enough to cover his sharp eyes. Perhaps to make up for his wiry build, Melvin carried two guns on his hip and was quick to display them to anyone who was interested.

Like the other three at the table, Jebediah Cobbler wasn't too interested in Melvin's guns. After sitting to Melvin's left for most of the night, Jebediah had developed the habit of nodding mindlessly when Melvin talked just to mask the fact that he wasn't listening. Although Jeb had the strong build and bright eyes of a younger man, he had the termperment of someone much older. He spoke with experience at times and seemed like easy pickings at others. That was a dangerous combination at any card table and this was no exception.

"All right, Clint," Melvin said. "Your deal."

Clint accepted the deck that was handed over to him and shuffled. "Normally, I'm more of a five-card draw sort of man, but you fellows have had a bad influence on me."

"Stud is a real man's game," Abe said.

Clint nodded. "My sentiments exactly. Stud it is." With

that, Clint flipped one card facedown to each of the players. After that, Clint dealt another card faceup to each man.

Abe wound up with the ten of clubs while Melvin got the king of hearts. The jack of spades landed in front of Jeb and Clint dealt himself the ace of spades.

Clint took a quick study of each of their faces before he even bothered to look at his own hole card. That one turned out to be the four of spades. "I'll bet five dollars," Clint said.

After the long night of gambling, Abe had become the easiest face to read of them all. He hadn't been drinking too much, but his emotions were out there for all to see no matter how much he tried to hide them. When he looked down at his card this time, he merely grunted before tossing out enough to cover the bet.

Melvin was next in line and took a few seconds to study the card he'd been dealt. The smirk on his face was there as always, but twitched just a little as he threw in enough to cover Abe's wager. "Guess I'll call as well," he said.

"Game's never the same without you," Clint said. "What about you, Jeb?"

The man at Clint's right would have been easier to read, but the expression on his face was always somewhat sour. Clint couldn't tell if that was Jeb's way of keeping to himself or if he always thought the worst about his situation. It worked to his advantage more often than not.

"Five, you say?"

"That's the bet," Melvin chimed in. "If it's too much for you, give up and go home."

Furrowing his brow, Jeb seemed to be considering that very thing. At least, he was until Melvin opened his mouth again.

"While you're home," Melvin said, "you can slip into a pretty little dress and bake me a cake."

Although Jeb wasn't the fighting sort, Clint could feel the other man's temper flaring like heat lightning crackling through a cloudy sky. "Don't let him bait you," Clint said without trying to sound like he was doing the same thing. "Just play the card you've got."

But Jeb didn't seem to hear a word Clint said as he threw in his money and glared over at Melvin. "I'm in."

Melvin smiled and nodded. "That's a good boy!"

Before those two could say anything else, Clint dealt the next round of cards. The queen of spades dropped in front of Abe. Melvin got the ace of diamonds and Jeb was on the receiving end of the seven of spades. Clint dropped the queen of diamonds for himself.

"Plenty of pain on the table," Melvin said. "But it looks like I'm at the top of the totem pole for now."

"So go ahead and bet," Clint said in a tone that had an edge to it, but wasn't quite aggressive.

Melvin nodded and took the hint from the one man at the table he hadn't been able to bully. "I bet fifteen dollars." After he tossed out the money, he stared at Jeb as if he'd just drawn a line in the sand.

Jeb took a look at his hole card.

"Still the same as it was a minute ago," Melvin snapped.

Plainly flustered, Jeb clenched his jaw shut and stared at the small pile of money at the middle of the table. A blind man could see that he wanted to fold, but he still couldn't quite get himself to toss his cards away.

Letting out a breath, Melvin shifted in his chair to look at Abe. "I'm hungry. Wouldn't a nice cake be good right about now?"

Abe chuckled, but tried not to be too loud about it.

"I enjoy the sweet frost too," Melvin continued. "What about you, Clint?"

"I'd enjoy some quiet while I deal."

Melvin nodded and bit his tongue. The way he glanced over at Jeb, however, spoke volumes.

"Raise it to thirty," Jeb said. Before he could think twice or change his mind, he pushed in his money.

Clint was sitting behind the biggest stack of cash and chips at the moment, so he called the bet.

Abe shook his head and shoved his cards toward the rest of the deck. "You stop dealing me this shit, Adams, and I'll play."

"Maybe next time," Clint replied with a smirk.

But Melvin had yet to take his eyes off Jeb. He glared at the other man the way a cat glared at a sleeping mouse. "How about we make this really interesting?"

TWO

"Before you boys get too carried away, how about a drink?"

That question came from a part of the saloon that was away from Clint's table. The one who'd asked it was not only the woman who kept the books for the saloon, but also its namesake.

Brooke Abernathy was a tall brunette with flowing hair and more curves than a wandering stream. With a voice that was colored with a smooth taste of a Southern accent, she could have said just about anything and it would sound good enough to send a chill down a man's spine.

"I'm parched," Clint said in an attempt to break up some of the tension at his table.

Standing behind Clint and Jeb, she placed a hand on each man's shoulder and leaned down to make it seem she was about to whisper in their ears. Some of her hair spilled over her shoulders to tickle both men's necks.

"Don't let Melvin here get the better of you," she said jokingly. "And don't let him talk you to death either." When she said that, she gave Jeb's shoulder a little squeeze.

"How about some coffee?" Clint asked.

6

"To hell with that," Abe grunted. "I'll take a beer."

"It's almost nine in the morning," Brooke reminded him.

"That mean all the beer's dried up?"

She rolled her eyes and straightened up. "One beer and three coffees," she said before anyone else could amend their order. As she turned to leave, she let her hand stay on Clint's shoulder a little longer. That hand drifted along the back of his neck before finally coming free at the last possible moment.

"So what's it going to be?" Clint asked. "You want to call Jeb's raise or not?"

Some of the wind that had been in Melvin's sails moments ago was no longer there. Whether that could be credited to Brooke or Clint was unclear. Either way, he wasn't nearly as excited when he said, "I'll call it, don't you worry."

Melvin pushed in enough to cover the bet and not a cent more.

"All right then," Clint said. "Let's see what else we've got."

Melvin was dealt the deuce of hearts and Jeb got the eight of diamonds. Clint wound up with a four of clubs to match the four of spades that was facedown in front of him. Although he didn't show it, Clint had a dramatic change of heart regarding his future in that hand when he saw that second four.

"Ace-king still bets," Clint announced.

As far as Clint could tell, that deuce hadn't helped Melvin in the least. Jeb was still unreadable since he seemed to be put off his balance by Melvin's constant needling.

"How much you got left?" Melvin asked.

Jeb didn't answer right away, but his eyes took on a more serious glint. After letting out a breath, he rummaged through the mix of cash and chips in front of him. "Looks like just over two hundred and fifty."

Melvin winked and said, "Then I'll bet. Make it . . . two hundred and fifty." His fingers sifted through what he had, which was mostly cash. The chips that he'd been given at the start of the game were mainly in Jeb's and Clint's piles. It was one of the few things that Melvin didn't regularly gab about.

"You're just steaming because of those three queens I got a few hands ago," Jeb moaned.

Without missing a beat, Melvin cocked his head and replied, "One way to find out."

Like a guardian angel, Brooke appeared with the drinks just as Jeb seemed ready to lunge across the table and rip that arrogant smirk off Melvin's face. "Here you go, boys," she said while setting down a cup of hot coffee in front of Clint, Jeb, and Melvin. "I'll be right back with your beer, Abe. That is, unless you'd rather come over to the bar so I can serve you?"

Abe didn't even budge to get another look at Brooke in the dark-blue dress that hugged her breasts like a second skin. "I don't want to miss a second of this," he said.

Turning to Clint, she asked, "Is there anything else I can do?"

"I don't think so, darlin'," Abe grunted.

But she kept her eyes on Clint. "Anything else you need?"

Since she looked to Clint as the most level-headed player to frequent the Georgia Peach in some time, he knew exactly what the look in Brooke's eyes meant. She could sense the tension as well and wanted to be sure that she wasn't about to be pulled into the middle of another brawl.

Letting out a measured breath, Jeb shoved in nearly everything he had. Doing that caused the ends of his mouth to drop as if they were both attached to sinking anchors. Looking down, he saw there were only two chips left.

"Now that's a pitiful sight," Melvin said through a poorly stifled laugh.

"We should be fine," Clint assured her. He shifted his glance across the table and added, "Isn't that right?"

Melvin raised his hands as if he was surrendering to the law. The grin on his face was slicker than a fish's backside.

Before another word could be said, Clint collected his own cards into a neat stack. "And just to keep an eye on things, I'll devote all my attention to dealing the final card."

"That's a fancy way of folding, is it?" Melvin chided.

"It certainly is." And before Melvin could tack on another comment, Clint added, "That all right with you?"

"Fine, Adams. Just fine." Although Melvin still wasn't eager to toss his barbs at Clint, he didn't seem any less inclined to leave Jeb alone.

And no matter how much Clint could sympathize with Jeb for being shoved around by an asshole like Melvin, that was all a part of poker. Things had a way of evening themselves out around a card table. At the very least, the men who didn't belong could learn something when they were eventually weeded out.

"Last card," Clint said. "Remember, fellas, this is supposed to be a friendly game."

As if bucking against that very statement, the king of spades landed in front of Melvin's spot. The moment he saw that king lying beside the other king in his hand, Melvin grinned like the devil himself.

Jeb twitched when the ten of hearts was dropped in front of him, but didn't say a word about it.

Rubbing his hands together, Melvin looked back and forth between Jeb and the sad little stack of chips in front of him.

"Pair of kings bets," Clint said to move things along before Melvin dragged it out much further.

"Tell you what," Melvin said with a smug grin. "I'll check it to you just to be a gentleman."

Jeb was thinking it over when he was interrupted by Melvin's grating voice.

"After all, far be it from me to intrude on time that you could be using to whip up that cake you promised me."

Clint recognized the look in Jeb's eyes all too well. Although that look seemed strange on Jeb's face, it was all too common when a game of poker was carried this far.

It was a look that always meant trouble.

THREE

Slowly, Jeb placed his hands flat upon the table in front of him. It was only then that Clint realized the sour-faced man was inching toward the gun strapped around his waist. Truth be told, Clint had all but forgotten that Jeb was wearing a gun at all. The weapon was an older-model Smith & Wesson, but it could get the job done well enough.

"You don't need to bet anything," Clint reminded him.

But Jeb wasn't listening. In fact, he didn't even seem to have noticedthàt anyone else had spoken.

"Jebediah," Clint said in a sharper tone that surprised even himself.

Clint's voice was more like a father snapping at a child, but it cut through the fog in Jeb's skull and brought the other man's eyes toward him. Lowering his voice a bit, Clint said, "He checked to you. There's no need to bet anything if you don't want to."

After a few moments, Jeb moved his hands again. "No, there's something I want to do," he said warily. "Since there's no other way to shut his mouth, I guess there's nothing else but for me to do it."

All this time, Melvin had had the good sense to keep quiet for a change. Now, he leaned back in his chair so that

11

his own hand could get closer to the pistol that he kept at his side. Like Jeb's weapon, that gun was spotted with rust and clunky as hell, but it was a gun all the same.

Jeb's hands snapped into a quick series of motions that put both Clint and Melvin on the edges of their seats. But rather than make a move toward his pistol, Jeb tugged the gold band off his left finger.

"This is worth at least another fifty," Jeb said with resignation.

"God damn," Abe said with a hearty laugh. "I thought for sure you were gonna skin that pistol of yours."

But Jeb wasn't through yet. He also took the watch from his pocket, as well as a silver cross that had been hanging around his neck. "That should bring me up to a hundred. My horse is outside and I'll wager that as well."

As much as Clint wanted to warn Jeb against getting in over his head, that was all a part of the game. Besides, if the other man hadn't listened to him yet, there was no reason for him to start now. Since Clint had dealt all the cards of that hand, he set the deck down and watched the rest of the show.

Just to be on the safe side, however, Clint shifted in his seat so he could draw his own modified Colt if the need should arise.

Melvin leaned back in his seat as well. Now, there was a thoughtful look on his face as he tapped his chin with one finger. Not once did he take his eyes off the man to his left. In fact, he was staring at him so hard that he practically burned a hole through Jeb's shirt.

"I've got two kings showing, but you know that already," Melvin said to himself more than to anyone else. "You've got a whole lot of nothing and are trying to push me out. Hold on now." Leaning forward, Melvin glanced at Jeb's cards and then looked back up at the man. "Spread those out so I can get a better look."

"They're the same as they were a few minutes ago," Jeb said with a grin.

Clint and Abe laughed at Jeb's sudden display of wit as Melvin nodded slowly.

"Just do as I asked," Melvin grunted. "I got a right to see the cards that are faceup."

Jeb reached down and spread out the cards so Melvin could see them all. Just like before, the jack and seven of spades lay beneath the eight of diamonds and the ten of hearts.

"Ah," Melvin said. "You want me to think you pulled that gut-shot straight out of your ass? Is that what you're trying to do?"

"I made my wager and showed my cards," Jeb replied. "You can call or fold."

"How much you think that broken-down horse of yours is worth?" Melvin asked.

Before Jeb could answer that, Clint cut in with, "You mean that fine mare out front? That's a fine piece of horse-flesh and I've seen more than enough to know what I'm talking about."

Although that was s slight exaggeration, Clint was more than happy to help strengthen Jeb's case. Besides, the look he got from Melvin was priceless.

Clint wasn't the only one to think so, since Abe also chimed in. "I was about to offer a couple hundred for that animal myself."

"All right, all right," Melvin snapped. "I'll put in the rest of my pile here. Is that enough for you?"

"There's less than the price of a broken-down horse there," Jeb pointed out.

"You don't think that's enough to cover the bet?"

"Not by a long shot."

The longer Melvin stared at Jeb, the narrower his gaze became. Finally, he was glaring at Jeb through angry slits.

"You just want to make me fold. You'd really get a thrill out of that, wouldn't you?"

"I'm just playing my hand."

"Speaking of which," Abe said, "how about we wrap this up while we're still young?"

"That's some fine talk considering that I've got most of your money here in front of me," Melvin growled. Shifting back to face Jeb, he said, "Fine. But if you think you're going to push me out of this, you can go straight to hell."

As Melvin's hand went to his hip, Clint almost drew his Colt out of pure reflex. But instead of drawing his pistol, Melvin dug in his pocket and fished out a folded piece of paper. When he slapped the paper down onto the heaping stack of chips and money, Melvin smiled as if he'd just won a war.

"What's that?" Jeb asked.

"It's a deed for one of my claims. One of my finer claims, I might add. That's a hell of a lot more valuable than that mangy horse and all your cheap jewelry, but I'm willing to put it up just to shut your damn mouth."

Jeb reached out and took the deed. Unfolding it, he quickly read through some of the print. "This is for a spot up on Farewell Mountain?"

"The same spot where I pulled out the money to finance this very game," Melvin proclaimed. "And if that's not good enough, you can go to—"

"Yeah, yeah," Clint interrupted. "We heard you the first time. But there's no way for us to know if this deed is worth the paper it's printed on."

"What the hell are you, Adams?" Melvin groused. "Are you Jeb's lawyer?" Shifting so he was looking straight at Jeb, he added, "Or did he just bribe you with those cakes he loves to bake so much?"

"I'll take the bet," Jeb said.

Melvin's arrogant grin reappeared on his face as he said, "Fine and dandy. Let's see if you can beat this." With that, Melvin flipped over his hole card, which was the ace of clubs. He arranged it to go alongside his other ace and then looked up proudly.

"If I couldn't have beat whatever you were holding," Jeb said, "I wouldn't have accepted that worthless deed you offered." When he turned over the nine of diamonds, Jeb put on a smug grin of his own.

FOUR

To say that Melvin was a bit surprised would have been like saying the Pacific Ocean was just a bit wet.

"You cheated," Melvin wheezed. "That's the only explanation."

Clint was doing a fairly good job of keeping his smile down to an acceptable level, but it wasn't easy. Abe, on the other hand, was slapping his knee and letting out a belly laugh that filled the entire saloon.

"It's a straight," Clint said. "That's all the explanation you need."

"It is a straight," Jeb declared as he leaned forward to make sure his words stung even harder when they hit Melvin's ears. "And the last time I checked, a straight still beat two pair."

"You're goddamn right it does!" Abe chuckled. Lifting his glass, he shouted, "Here's to ya!"

Melvin's eyes looked about ready to pop out of their sockets. When he let out his breath, he dropped back into his chair. "You drew me in, knowing you'd get those cards."

Jeb was smiling even wider now. And just when it looked like he couldn't smile any more, he started raking in his chips. Once he got his arms wrapped around the bulk of the pot, he looked so happy that he might bust.

"You did most of the work yourself," Jeb said.

But Melvin kept shaking his head. "You cheated. Must've been. Either that or you arranged to get those cards dealt to you."

"Now you're calling me a cheater," Clint said with an edge in his voice. "Now's about the time where you shut your mouth and take your loss like a man."

"Bullshit!" Melvin said as he slapped his hand down against the table so hard that it spilled every stack of chips that was on it. "He was bluffing me. I knew it. Why the hell else would I toss in all that money?"

Looking up from his winnings, Jeb said, "You know something? You're right. I was bluffing. Right up until I got the last card I needed to fill out my straight."

Even before that entire sentence left Jeb's mouth, Clint knew where it was headed. He also knew he would need to act quickly if he was to prevent a whole lot of blood from being spilt at that table.

The moment Melvin pushed away from the table, Clint did the same. Both men reached for their guns at the same time, but it was Clint who cleared leather first. The modified Colt came up in a flicker of movement and was pointed at Melvin's face before anyone else even knew there was trouble.

"You don't want to do that, Melvin," Clint said in an unwavering voice. "Trust me."

Melvin had his gun in hand and was starting to draw when he found himself staring down the barrel of Clint's Colt. Opening his hand to allow the gun to drop back into its holster, he put on a shaky grin and lifted his arms until they were both over the table.

"Do what?" Melvin asked.

Jeb was frozen with his arms wrapped around his winnings. Now that he had a chance to see what was about to happen, he began easing away from the table. As he did, a few chips along with some silver dollars clattered to the floor.

"The game's over," Clint said. "Time for everyone to go home before we get too cross from staying up so late."

Without paying any mind to the guns or the fierce intentions written across some of the players' faces, Brooke walked right up to the table. "Clint's right. You boys are getting a little cranky, so why don't you go and get some sleep? The cards will still be here later on."

Melvin nodded and scooted back. "Can I get up or are you gonna shoot me?"

As Clint got to his feet, he eased the Colt back into its holster. His right hand stayed close to the pistol while his other collected what was left of his money.

"Now that's a hell of a way to end the night," Abe grunted. "I would've preferred to win back some of my money, but I guess the show was worth some of it."

Clint nodded toward Abe and replied, "Maybe next time."

"Yeah. Next time." Since he didn't have any money to collect, Abe stumbled out of the saloon.

Melvin shook his head and backed away from the table. "I still say I was cheated."

"Losers tend to say that an awful lot. Either prove it, get a witness, or shut your mouth."

"All right, Adams. No need for hard feelings. At least," Melvin added while shooting a glance over to Jeb, "not between you and me."

Staying in his spot with his hand still close to his gun, Clint said, "Brooke, cash out Jeb's chips."

"Already ahead of you," she said while handing a neat stack of bills to Jeb.

For Melvin, seeing that money handed over was like hearing the last nail being driven into a coffin. He rolled his eyes and huffed away from the table, muttering something or other under his breath. When he was gone, the rest of the saloon let out the breath they'd been holding.

"I appreciate that, Mr. Adams," Jeb said after stuffing his money into a couple different pockets.

"Don't mention it. I think everyone here knows that ol' Melvin was more bark than bite. Just be careful going home with all that money."

"I will. If there is any trouble, I should be able to handle it." As he said that last part, Jeb patted the old gun at his side.

"Even so," Clint said, "be careful."

Jeb nodded and walked out of the saloon.

Clint started to follow him, but was held back when Brooke reached out to grab his elbow.

"Why don't I come with you?" she asked.

"Are you worried about Jeb," Clint replied as he wrapped his arm around hers, "or are you just trying to get me alone?"

She smirked at him and said, "I guess we'll just have to see how your luck holds up."

FIVE

Clint had only met Jebediah Cobbler two days ago. Although he was a nice fellow, Jeb was still one of many nice fellows who had traded bets and swapped stories with Clint over the years. Even so, Clint didn't want to see Jeb get killed on his way down the wrong street with his pockets full of money.

And Clint wasn't the only one concerned for Jeb's safety. Brooke usually accompanied Clint when they were both leaving the Georgia Peach. This time, however, her eyes were more focused on Jeb and she was more than willing to keep as quiet as Clint as they walked through the streets of Mud Foot.

Jeb was in a hurry to leave the saloon, and was in an even bigger hurry to get home. That was just fine with the two people who were following him half a block away. As Jeb rounded a corner, he shot a glance over his shoulder and completely failed to see Clint and Brooke standing on the boardwalk.

"Is he close to his house?" Clint asked after they'd rounded the same corner.

Brooke nodded. "Right in front of it."

"Good."

20

She looked over at Clint and patted his chest with the palm of her hand. "You've got a big heart, Clint Adams."

"I just didn't want to see anything ugly happen while I was still about," he said with a shrug. "Now that he's at his house, he can fend for himself."

Clint's arm slipped around Brooke's waist to pull her close as he once again started walking down the street. "I guess that just leaves me with one other person who needs an escort."

"Needs?" she asked with a sharp edge to her voice. "As I recall, you've been more than willing to follow me home the last few nights."

"That was then," Clint said as he stopped and turned to face her. "This is now and I distinctly remember you asking to come along with me."

Although she still maintained the appearance of being on edge, Brooke had no problem with stepping closer to Clint and leaning against his chest. Her dark hair fell over her face and her eyes all but closed as she stretched out to put her mouth close to his ear.

"I guess I did enjoy watching you tonight," she whispered.

"Really? Maybe I should lose at poker more often."

When she smiled, Brooke's full lips brushed against Clint's earlobe. Her breath came out in a slow, warm purr. "The way you stood up to that windbag. The way you handled yourself. The way you stuck up for Jeb and chased those others out before they worked up the nerve to make a move. It made my blood turn hot."

Clint's hands slid along her rounded hips. Before his hands drifted any higher or lower, he had to remind himself that they were both still standing on the street. Just because it wasn't the busiest section of town didn't mean that someone couldn't walk by at any moment.

"It's been a long night," Clint said. "I thought I'd just go back to my hotel and get some sleep."

Brooke's head snapped back a little so she could look into his eyes. "Back to your hotel? Alone?"

"I find that's the best way for me to sleep."

"Oh, no, you don't," she said while standing beside him and dragging him along the boardwalk by the hand. "I didn't serve you the strongest coffee I could make just for you to curl up and go to sleep."

"And here I thought you were just being polite."

Tossing her hair over one shoulder, she shot Clint a playful look. "You just like to see me squirm. I take back anything I said about you being a good man, Clint. You're devious."

Clint allowed himself to be dragged behind her. "But you look so pretty when you squirm."

Before Brooke could respond to that, they passed by an older couple who were on their way to catch breakfast. The man had a thick head of silvery hair and tipped his hat. His wife wore an ever-present smile and nodded to Clint and Brooke.

"Fine morning, isn't it?" the older man asked with a wide smile.

"It sure is," Brooke said while trying to keep the couple from seeing the flush that had come to her cheeks.

Clint tipped his hat and returned their smiles. "And it looks like it's only going to get better."

SIX

Strictly speaking, Clint was staying at a hotel not too far from the Georgia Peach. The truth of the matter was that he hadn't rumpled the sheets of that bed he was renting since he'd met Brooke Abernathy. The voluptuous brunette had occupied most of Clint's time when he wasn't at a poker table, marking his stay in Mud Foot a whole lot better than he'd been expecting.

Now, Clint was discovering that she had been speaking the truth when she'd told him that her blood was running hot. The moment he slammed the door of her house shut, Clint was practically knocked against a wall as Brooke pressed herself against him.

"That walk home was torture," she whispered. "I've been thinking about getting my hands on you for hours."

While she talked about it, Clint was letting his hands do his speaking for him. He quickly pulled open the buttons holding the upper portion of her dress together so he could slip his fingers beneath the soft material. The bare skin underneath was even softer.

Brooke wore a thin black camisole under her dress, which now clung tightly to her proud, full breasts. She let

out a sigh as Clint rubbed the palms of his hands along the
sides of her breasts and worked his way to her nipples.

Just as she reached up to place her hands on top of his,
Clint eased them down a little further to trace along her
sides. As he slid his hands over her ribs, he pulled her dress
down until it was bunched around her waist.

"There now," he said while leaning in to nibble her
neck. "That's just the squirming I was talking about."

Sure enough, Brooke shifted her hips from side to side
in a way similar to a cat twitching its tail. She leaned her
head back and closed her eyes as a soft, satisfied smile
eased onto her face. "You keep touching me like that and
you'll get enough squirming to last a lifetime."

"Let's just see about that." After lingering a few more
seconds, Clint moved his hands further down, savoring the
curve of her hips before sampling the inviting slope of her
buttocks.

By the time she felt her dress fall to the floor, Brooke
was on her tiptoes. Part of that was so she could kiss more
of Clint's neck, and another part was an instinct that made
her arch her back as Clint's hands got closer to her thighs.

Underneath her skirts, Brooke was wearing nothing but
a black-lace garter belt that hooked onto a pair of matching
silk stockings. Her legs were slender and soft to the touch.
As Clint eased his hands between them, he could feel that
she was warm, wet, and ready for him.

"Those are my favorite stockings," he told her.

"I know." Her eyes drank in the sight of his chest as she
pulled open his shirt. Her hands worked quickly to un-
buckle his pants so she could wrap her fingers around his
stiff cock. "And this is my favorite."

"Then by all means, help yourself."

And that was exactly what she did. As Brooke lowered
herself onto her knees, she cupped him in one hand while
using the other to guide him between her lips. She slipped

her tongue out to glide along the bottom of his penis before swallowing him whole.

Now it was Clint's turn to arch his back as he slid his fingers through Brooke's thick, dark hair. She didn't need much guidance as she bobbed her head back and forth, so Clint kept his hand in place just to be certain she wouldn't stop.

Just as he was approaching the point of no return, Clint eased her back and helped her back onto her feet.

"What's the matter?" she asked with a pouting look in her eyes. "Didn't you like that?"

The only answer he needed to give was picking her up and carrying her to the bed.

Along the way, Brooke wrapped her legs around him and grabbed onto Clint's shoulders for support. Even before they'd made it to the bedroom, she'd opened her thighs a bit more and positioned herself so that Clint's rigid penis slipped partway into her.

"That's it," she purred. "That's what I've been waiting for."

Although the bed was in sight, Clint kept hold of her and turned to put her back against a tall wardrobe in one corner of the room. "Is that what you want?" he asked while staring straight into her eyes.

Excitement flashed across Brooke's face at the edge in Clint's voice. "Yes, it is. Give it to me."

"You've got to say please," Clint said as he made slow circles with his hips in a way that brushed his cock in and out of her while also grazing against the sen sitive skin of her clitoris.

At first, Brooke's eyes had been closed. When she felt his erection touch a certain spot, however, her eyes shot open and her breath caught in her throat. With effort, she pushed out the words, "Please, Clint. Please!"

Unable to torture himself or Brooke any longer, Clint

thrust his hips forward and buried his cock inside her. Both of them let out loud, relieved moans. As Clint began pumping in and out, those moans turned into primal, rhythmic grunts.

Brooke kept one hand wrapped around the back of Clint's neck while reaching out to grab hold of the wardrobe with the other. Once she'd steadied herself even better, she started grinding her hips in time to Clint's thrusts. Between the insistent movements of her body and the excitement running through her blood, sweat was pouring down Brooke's neck, plastering her camisole to her breasts and stomach.

Clint cupped her backside in both hands and moved her away from the wardrobe. Luckily, the bed was close by because his knees were already growing weak from the way Brooke expertly shifted her hips. The moment he set her onto the mattress, Clint felt Brooke stretch out and wrap her legs around him even tighter.

From there, Clint clasped both of her hands in his and pinned them to the pillows close to her head. Once more showing her wide-eyed excitement, Brooke arched her back and pumped her hips furiously as Clint plunged into her.

As the bed rocked against the bedroom wall and Brooke moaned loudly in his ear, Clint knew he'd been the biggest winner at that poker table.

SEVEN

Jebediah Cobbler felt like he was the luckiest man to ever walk out of the Georgia Peach. Come to think of it, he felt like the luckiest man in town. When he patted his pockets, which were fat with more money than he'd ever had at once, he felt like the luckiest man in Montana.

His little house was just about to fall out of his hands before he'd had his windfall. Until this very morning, Jeb had been almost too heartbroken to be in his house since it was just about to be reclaimed by the local bankers.

Now, he sat on his porch without the ever-present knot in his belly and with more than enough cash to make his problems go away. As the sun shone down on him that day, there wasn't a thing under it that could have wiped the smile off Jeb's face. At least, he'd thought that until he saw the man come walking up to his fence and kick at the gate.

Jeb was still smiling, but it was an uncomfortable sort of smile that did nothing to hide the fear in his eyes. "Hello there," he said to the man at his gate. "I . . . uhh . . . didn't expect to see you."

"Yeah," Abe snarled. "I'll just bet you didn't."

Even though he'd come to a stop, Abe was still wobbling back and forth as if he was on a moving train. His right hand was grabbing onto the closest fence post he could reach while his left hand was wrapped around a mostly empty bottle.

Abe's hair was a tussled mess and was so greasy, nobody could say for certain what color it was. His skin was smudged with dirt and sweat trickled down his face.

"Sure is hot today," Jeb said weakly.

"Fuck you," Abe growled just a bit too loudly. When he looked around to see if anyone was nearby, he almost fell over. Eventually, he managed to get his eyes refocused upon Jeb.

Getting to his feet, Jeb stood in front of his door. "What can I do for you?"

"You can give me back my money, that's what."

"Pardon me?"

"Don't pull that shit on me, Cobbler! I lost every goddamn cent to my name in that card game and you've got it."

"I wasn't the only one who—"

"Maybe not the only one," Abe cut in. "But you sure as hell got the most of it." The more Abe talked, the more slurred his voice became. His eyelids were heavy, which forced him to stare angrily out at the world through puffy slits.

Sensing the rage in Abe's voice, Jeb took a step back and bumped against his front door. "Take it easy, Abe. You're drunk." As he talked, Jeb patted the air in front of him.

While that motion was intended to calm Abe down, it acted more like dry wood that had been tossed onto a fire.

"You goin' for yer gun?" Abe shouted. "You wan' to shoot me rather than pay back what you stole?"

"I didn't steal anything! I didn't cheat!"

Abe started to walk forward and nearly fell flat onto his face when he tripped over the closed gate. After clumsily regaining his balance, he all but tore the gate off its hinges. "You think that's funny?"

A smile hadn't even begun to cross Jeb's face. "No!"

"You were smilin' plenty wide before. I bet you was sitting there thinking about all the wool you pulled over my eyes!"

"I didn't even win that money off of you," Jeb said quickly as his brain struggled for a way out of this mess. "Melvin was the one who won it when he caught that full house and you had three jacks. Remember that?"

"Course I remember," Abe said, even though the confusion in his eyes told a very different story. With his eyes fixed upon Jeb, Abe's head was the only part of him that remained steady as he worked his way toward the little house. "But it was you that walked out of there. An' you walked out with my money! You even had that gunfighter walk you out like your own personal guard."

After taking a few more steps, Abe teetered on the balls of his feet and added, "Melvin was right. You ain't nothing but a little bitch."

Jeb did his best to stand up straight, but it was difficult considering how petrified he was. "What do you want from me?"

"I want my goddamn money."

"You lost it in a fair game."

Abe lunged forward like he'd been launched from a cannon. Part of that was due to the rage causing every muscle in his body to jump under his skin. Another part was due to his first stumbling steps causing the rest of his body to move forward on its own momentum.

Reaching out with both arms, Abe was able to push away from a post supporting the house's front awning while also getting a sloppy hold on Jeb's shirt. Pulling himself and Jeb closer together, Abe spit stinking breaths at the other man as he said, "Don't tell me that! I want my money!"

"I can't, Abe."

"What?"

"I said I can't give that money back," Jeb repeated as he

knocked away Abe's hand and fumbled behind him to open the door.

Abe was just drunk enough to be pushed away by Jeb's flailing arms. When Jeb managed to get through the front door and slam it shut again, Abe was still on the porch with a stunned look on his face.

"How the fuck could you lose all that money?" Abe shouted as he tried to figure out where Jeb had gone.

"I didn't lose it," Jeb shouted through the closed door.

Now that he realized where Jeb's voice was coming from, Abe stumbled forward so he could punch and kick at the door. "Then hand it over! It's mine! It's all I got!"

"I told you, it's spoken for!"

"Where could it go?"

"I need to pay for this house and the land it's on, or the bankers will claim it!"

As Abe tried to make sense of the words still echoing through his drunken mind, his eyes darted in odd patterns as if he was watching a couple flies racing around his head. Not much of what Jeb told him sank in, but he'd heard enough to stoke the rage in him even higher.

"I don't give a damn about none of that. If you ain't coming out," Abe said as he slammed his bottle against the house, "then I'm comin' in after ya!"

EIGHT

The steps pounded against the front porch like train wheels clattering over the tracks. That same pattern of noise was continued when the person making it reached the front door and started rapping on it like a woodpecker.

Brooke pulled the door open and almost had to dodge an incoming set of knuckles as the woman outside kept up her furious knocking. When she saw that the door was open, the older woman's smile returned.

"Oh, thank goodness you're here," she said.

Brooke nodded. "What's the matter, Sandra?"

"There's a commotion over at Jebediah Cobbler's. The last time I saw him, he was headed into that saloon where you work."

"Right. He was there all night and left just a few hours ago. What's the problem?"

Sandra kept glancing over her shoulder and then looking back at Brooke. Every time she did so, it set her back as far as spitting out what she wanted to say. "I . . . I'm not sure, but I think someone was trying to kick in Jebediah's door."

"I know how he feels," Brooke replied with a grin.

Just then, Sandra realized she still had her hand raised

as if she was going to start knocking again at any moment. Also, her entire body was perched on tiptoe like a cat that was ready to jump. She did her best to ease up a little, but still looked awfully jittery.

Until now, Clint had respected Brooke's rushed request and kept out of sight. In a town as small as Mud Foot, Brooke already had a mark against her just for working in a saloon. Being seen with a man in her home so blatantly was a mess that she didn't want to get into.

But even from where he'd been hiding, Clint could hear the desperation in Sandra's voice. He'd also had more than enough time to make himself presentable.

"What seems to be the problem?" Clint asked as he stepped into the doorway next to Brooke.

For a moment, Brooke looked upset that he was in plain sight. But Sandra was not at all worried about being proper just then. In fact, she seemed very happy to see Clint step into view.

"Mr. Adams," Sandra said. "I was hoping to find you here."

"You were?" Brooke asked.

"There's some trouble at Jebediah Cobbler's," the older woman repeated, ignoring the flustered look on Brooke's face. "Do you know him?"

"Well," Clint grumbled, "I guess you could say that."

"Then do you think you might lend a hand? Jebediah might need someone with your . . . talents." When she said that last part, Sandra glanced down at the gun belt strapped around Clint's waist.

"What kind of trouble did you say he was in?" Clint asked.

"A man was trying to kick in his door. He seemed drunk and very upset."

Looking to Brooke, Clint asked, "You think it's Melvin?"

Brooke looked to Sandra. "Was he a skinny fellow with dark hair?"

The older woman was shifting on her feet and getting more nervous by the second. "He had dark hair, but he wasn't skinny. Please, something needs to be done quickly or it'll be too late to do anything at all. I think I can hear the yelling from here."

Clint stepped outside and could hear the shouting with his own ears. Although he couldn't be sure of the exact words that were being shouted, Clint was certain of one thing. "That's not Melvin."

Sandra stepped aside to let Clint pass and then immediately fell into step behind him. "It looked like Jebediah's gate was broken. I think his front door might have been kicked in as well. I'm also certain I heard gunshots."

"Aw, hell," Clint groaned as he quickened his pace toward the street. He knew where Jeb's house was, especially since there was more than enough commotion to lead him straight to the source.

The scent of burnt gunpowder was in the air, and grew stronger as Clint hurried toward the little house at the end of its row. There wasn't much to see from where he was standing. Although the gate was broken and shattered glass littered the ground, there wasn't anything moving.

In fact, the scene was a little too still for Clint's liking. Considering that the front door was hanging half off its hinges, he just hoped that he wasn't already too late to be of any help.

NINE

As soon as Clint ran past the broken gate, he heard a loud thump from inside Jeb's house. Keeping one hand on his Colt, he jumped up the few stairs leading to the porch and ran to the front door. Just as he made out the shape of someone standing inside the house, Clint saw that person turn and swing a gun around to aim in his direction.

Clint didn't have to think about what he was doing. His reflexes were quick enough to position himself away from the open doorway while also drawing the modified Colt. The moment his back bumped against the wall beside the door, a shot barked from within the house.

"Who's there?" an angry, slurred voice hollered from inside.

Before Clint could answer, another shot was fired through the door.

Although Brooke had been following Clint, she hadn't been able to keep up with him thanks to the shoes she wore. She hadn't even made it through the gate when that first shot had been fired, and she had since managed to duck behind a tree at the edge of Jeb's property. With a few quick waves, Clint motioned for her to stay right where she was.

"What's going on in there?" Clint shouted.

"It's personal business, so keep yer goddamn nose out of it!"

"Abe?" Clint asked. "Is that you?"

"Who the hell's asking?"

"It's Clint Adams."

There was silence for a moment. Soon, a few irregular footsteps stomped toward the door.

"Where you hiding, Adams?"

Steeling himself, Clint eased himself to one side so he could peek through the door. He could immediately see that the inside of the house was tussled and smoky. Abe was standing there with a gun in his hand. It took a few seconds for his eyes to focus on Clint, but when they did, he brought his gun up and pulled his trigger.

Clint pulled his head back with time to spare before Abe managed to take his shot. The blast echoed within the house and a chunk of the door frame was blasted off. It might have come close to hitting Clint if he'd been standing on the opposite side of the door.

"You're drunk, Abe," Clint said. "What the hell are you doing in Jeb's house?"

"Yer damn right I'm drunk! I'm also broke!"

"That still doesn't answer my question."

After a good, long five seconds, Clint risked another peek around the door frame. He saw Abe standing there like a monkey that had been asked to do long division. Once Abe caught sight of him, however, the confusion left his eyes and he fired off another quick shot.

"All right," Clint said under his breath. "I've had enough of this."

With that, Clint hunched down and turned the corner in one smooth motion. Keeping his head low, he charged for Abe as another shot was fired through the air well above him. Clint's shoulder connected with Abe's gut and knocked the man back several steps.

In fact, it didn't take long before Clint realized that Abe

was stumbling without control and Clint was now stumbling with him. Clint managed to shove Abe back while regaining his own balance. As Abe slammed against a cabinet full of plates, Clint stood directly in front of him.

"Just what the hell is going on in here?" Clint asked. "Where's Jeb?"

"That son of a bitch owes me my money!"

"Yeah, yeah. I heard that much the first time. Where is he?"

Abe grumbled another bunch of nothing, which was too slurred to be understood. As he talked, he lifted his gun and let out a wheezing breath that reeked of liquor.

Clint slapped Abe's gun out of his hand without much effort. One good shove was all it took to knock Abe against the cabinet again. This time, he stayed put.

There wasn't much else to see inside the house. Although there were a few other rooms, it didn't look as if anyone was in them. "Jeb!" Clint shouted. "Where are you?"

Now that Abe wasn't swearing at the top of his lungs and shooting every couple of seconds, Clint was able to hear more voices coming from outside. They weren't coming from the front of the house, however. Instead, they were drifting in through a door in the kitchen that had probably creaked open thanks to a strong breeze.

". . . don't want to do this," one of those voices said.

Since Abe wouldn't have been able to find his own ass with both hands, Clint wasn't too worried about him finding where his gun had landed after being kicked. Besides, Abe was doing his best at the moment just to stay upright.

Clint headed toward the back door as quickly as he could, but without making too much noise. He was in a small kitchen that got most of its light through two small, square windows. After taking a glimpse through the closest of those windows, Clint knew he wasn't about to walk straight into a firing squad.

In fact, it looked as though there were only two men in back of the house. A few of the boards creaked under his boots as Clint positioned himself closer to the door, but the men out back were too preoccupied to notice something like that.

One of those men was Jeb and he was standing about five paces out of the house with his back to the door. The only other man out there was less than ten feet in front of Jeb. He was a tall, lanky fellow with messy black hair, dull eyes, and a mouth that seemed incapable of closing.

"You don't tell me what I want to do," the slack-jawed man said. He was carrying a shotgun, which was aimed in Jeb's general direction. Unfortunately, that was as good of an aim that was needed to kill a man with a shotgun at that range.

TEN

Jeb held out both hands, apparently unaware that Clint was right behind him. "I already told you, Matt. This is all a big mistake."

"Just shut your mouth and fetch that cash. We don't got a fancy house like this, so we need what's rightfully ours."

Clint stepped outside and placed a hand on Jeb's shoulder. Jeb almost jumped out of his boots, but let out a relieved breath when he saw who was behind him.

"Who're you?" Matt asked.

"My name's Clint Adams." Clint waited a moment to see if that would light any sort of spark behind Matt's nearly vacant eyes.

It didn't.

"This has gone far enough," Clint said. "Now put down that shotgun before it gets out of hand."

Jeb turned to shoot a surprised look at Clint. Rather than try to explain that he knew things had already gotten way out hand, Clint merely nodded. Keeping his hand on Jeb's shoulder, Clint moved the man aside so he could keep stepping forward.

"Your brother's inside," Clint said. "Why don't you collect him and get out of here?"

"We came here for a reason."

"I know, but he's drunk and you're . . ." Again, Clint stopped himself. At least, he paused just long enough for him to fit in a word that wouldn't be so guaranteed to rub Matt the wrong way. "You mean well, I'm sure."

"Abe?" Matt shouted. "Oh. There you are."

Clint heard the boards creak behind him, but it was too late. Abe rushed toward him like a charging bull and caught Clint in the small of his back with a wild punch.

That punch nearly took all the wind from Clint's lungs and almost caused him to lose his grip on the modified Colt. But even as he was staggering to one side and trying to suck in a breath, Clint managed to keep his gun in reach.

"Take whatever this asshole's got!" Abe shouted.

Matt nodded once and rushed forward to carry out his orders.

Glancing at each of the other three men, Jeb tried to back away from all of them at the same time. All he managed to do was back himself right into the back wall of his own house. Seeing as how Matt had at least four inches on him and was still carrying the shotgun, it was no wonder that Jeb was practically tripping over himself just to get away.

Clint had managed to turn halfway around before he felt Abe's arms wrap around his midsection. Those arms closed in a painful bear hug that lifted Clint completely off his feet. He was trapped at such an odd angle that it took him a moment to get his bearings. When he did, he realized just how much trouble he was in.

"Shoot this bastard, Matt," Abe grunted.

The moment Abe had spoken those words, Clint managed to slam a heel into Abe's knee. That was enough for Clint to get his own feet back on the ground again, but not quite enough to loosen Abe's hold. The man was still drunk as a skunk and had the strength of a lunatic to go along with it. Rather than try to bargain any longer, Clint swung around to face Abe while lashing out with a right hook.

Clint's punch had more momentum than a steam engine racing downhill. When his fist connected with Abe's face, he nearly took the drunk's head off his shoulders. The impact made a dull cracking sound and sent a spray of bloody spit through the air.

Abe's arms came loose immediately and he staggered back through the door and into the kitchen. This time, Clint followed him inside to make sure the other man was down for good.

"The ironic part of this," Clint said as he slammed his left fist into Abe's stomach, "is that I thought you had the best nature out of anyone at that card table."

Clint took a step back so he could get a look at Abe's face. When he did, he saw that the mix of anger and liquor was still too strong and there wasn't much hope of getting through it just yet. When Abe tried taking a swing at him, Clint ducked under it and delivered a second punch to Abe's gut.

Slouching forward while letting out a pained grunt, Abe caught Clint's knee square in the face. That straightened him back up again and sent him staggering back.

As much as he truly hated to do it, Clint lashed out with one more punch to Abe's bloody face. This one snapped the drunk's head back and dropped him like a sack of flour. The moment Abe's back hit the floor, he started snoring loudly.

Clint shook his head and turned to rush back outside. The moment he stepped through the door again, he nearly walked straight into a hailstorm of buckshot.

The shotgun's roar caught Clint off guard and froze in his mind as if that was the last thing he would ever hear. That sound filled his head and made his heart skip a beat. It was one of the sounds that made his mind sift through every moment in the blink of an eye.

Some men talked about their life flashing before their eyes.

This was one of those moments.

When the roar of the shotgun finally started to fade just a little, Clint was glad to feel the bite of pain in his left leg.

Pain meant that he was still alive.

At least, he was still alive for the moment.

The smoke was still billowing through the air when Clint regained his senses. He'd been hit in the upper thigh, but it wasn't more than a deep scratch. He could still stand up and that was all that mattered just then.

Matt stared dimly ahead, barely acknowledging that he'd just shot a man. Once he spotted Jeb trying to jump off the side of the porch, he shifted his aim and started squeezing the shotgun's second trigger.

Clint cleared leather and aimed his modified Colt at the hip. He took quick aim and pulled the trigger another fraction of a second later. As the Colt bucked against his palm, he already knew for certain where that bullet would go.

Sure enough, that chunk of hot lead chipped off a piece of meat on Matt's right forearm. The bullet's power was more than enough to knock Matt to that side and pull his aim way off target.

The second barrel of the shotgun belched out its smoky breath and sent its payload through the air. Rather than come anywhere close to Jeb, however, the buckshot slammed into the side of the house to shatter one of the small, square windows.

"Ow!" Matt groaned.

As Clint moved forward, he felt the pain from where he'd been hit. The blood rushing through his veins was more than enough to see him through that minor inconvenience.

Keeping his gun aimed at Matt, Clint reached out with his free hand to rip the shotgun from the other man's grasp. "Jeb, go find someone to haul these two assholes away."

Jeb nodded and scrambled around the other side of the house.

"Just so you know," Clint said to Matt, "if you so much as think of saying another word, you'll be having this shotgun for breakfast."

ELEVEN

Once things were wrapped up at Jeb's house, Clint wanted to wash his hands of all three of the men who had played with him at that card game. So far, Melvin was doing him the favor of staying out of sight and keeping his big mouth shut.

When Jeb approached him with hat in hand, however, Clint couldn't get himself to refuse the humble invitation.

"This is the best place to eat in town," Jeb said anxiously.

So far, Clint had only tasted the little place's rolls and he couldn't refute Jeb's claim.

It was a little restaurant sandwiched in between the Georgia Peach and a tailor's shop. The only reason Clint hadn't eaten there yet was because the restaurant's sign had faded completely away from staying out in the sun.

"What do you think, Mr. Adams?" Jeb asked. "How do you like it?"

Brooke was at their table as well and she leaned over to get some butter. "Clint will do anything for steak. That's his weakness." Glancing at him with a naughty little smirk, she added, "Well, one of them anyway."

If Jeb noticed anything going on between Clint and

Brooke, he gave no indication. Instead, he simply waited expectantly for Clint to answer his question for himself.

Holding a roll in one hand and a glass of water in the other, Clint said, "So far, so good."

Jeb smiled as if he'd just won another big hand of poker. "Great! After what you did for me, I figure it's the least I can do. You sure you won't take any reward money?"

"I didn't do anything to deserve a reward."

"You got shot."

"And since I came by to help of my own volition," Clint replied, "that isn't anyone's fault but mine."

"I'd say it's that idiot brother of Abe's fault," Brooke said. "He's the one that did the shooting."

"And he's also the one cooling his heels in a jail cell right now," Clint said. "Right along with his brother. I got my leg stitched up. There's a steak dinner on its way to my table and all's right with the world."

"Well, you can have steak for dinner, lunch, and breakfast for a month," Jeb said. "My treat."

Without hesitation, Clint said, "I'll take you up on that. At least, I will for supper tonight and breakfast tomorrow."

"Honestly, Mr. Adams. I can afford to—"

"It's not that, Jeb. I'll be leaving tomorrow morning."

"On account of this mess?"

"No. I'm just moving on. To be honest, I stayed a whole lot longer than I'd expected. This is a hell of a town." Feeling a pinch from the fresh stitches in his leg, Clint pressed his hand against the newest wound. "Hell of a town indeed."

Jeb looked put off by the news, but soon slipped into his normal, quiet mannerisms. "Where will you be headed?"

"South. It's been a while since I've seen a desert sunrise."

"That sounds beautiful," Brooke said.

"And quiet," Clint added with no small amount of enthusiasm. "Real quiet."

The smell of steaks being cooked drifted through the air as Jeb reached out to grab another hot roll. "Well, my offer stands for breakfast, so don't try to skip out of town too early. And whatever supplies you need, just let Earl over at the store know who you are and he'll put them on my account."

"Much obliged, Jeb. Maybe I can get back what I lost at that card game after all." Clint let that one hang in the air just long enough for Jeb to show some concern. He then let the man off the hook by laughing and giving his shoulder a nudge.

Their food was brought to them and all three started eating without a lot of conversation. Jeb was still jittery about everything that had happened. Brooke had yet to get more than a few minutes of sleep and Clint was just plain hungry.

After a few tender bites of steak had been followed by some baked potato and washed down with cool water, Clint was feeling much more sociable. While cutting off his next hunk of meat, Clint said, "You really should make sure that money is in a safe place."

Jeb nodded. "I'll be going to the bank later today."

"What then?" Brooke asked. "Do you have any big plans for your new windfall?"

"I sure do. I intend on buying my house and land outright. That's what kept me from just handing it all back when Abe and his brother came calling. Something about seeing them break up my place made me feel like I'd rather die than hand it over."

"Men do seem to find a whole lot of courage when they're defending their homes," Clint pointed out. "Sounds like you've got a nice future ahead of you."

"Sure. So long as them other two don't come back."

"They'll be in jail for a while after what they did. And once you've paid for your house, you won't have much left for Abe to steal."

"Besides," Brooke added, "those idiots were so drunk that you could tell them they got all your money and spent it and they'd be hard pressed to say otherwise."

"I'll drink to that," Jeb said as he lifted his glass.

Clint and Brooke followed suit and finished the rest of the meal with nothing more than a little friendly talk and some apple pie. Jeb invited Clint to stop by later for a cigar, but he declined. He didn't even pay another visit to the Georgia Peach.

After the time he'd had in Mud Foot, Clint was looking forward to a few nights sleeping under the stars with nobody to complicate things. Then again, it didn't take a whole lot of convincing for Brooke to lure him back to her house for one last good-bye.

TWELVE

Clint woke up before the sun cast its first light across the sky.

He woke up before Brooke had even opened her eyes.

He woke up before most of Mud Foot had even begun to stir.

Rather than wait for first light or bother with taking Jeb's offer for a free steak-and-eggs breakfast, Clint gathered his things and went to get Eclipse ready to go. The Darley Arabian stallion had been sleeping as well, but woke up plenty fast enough when he heard the familiar jangle of his saddle's buckle.

There were a few souls out and about when Clint finally rode out of town, but they hardly even noticed him leave. The sky was just starting to show the first streaks of purple that announced the coming of the dawn. Eclipse had traveled a few miles before that first light finally arrived.

Although Clint still had his mind set on heading toward the desert, he wasn't in any particular hurry. One thing in particular had altered his plan and that was the sight of the mountains looming to the west. He'd seen plenty of mountains in his day, but there was always something particularly breathtaking about the mountains when seen in

Montana. It was almost as if that part of the world had the best seat in the house where high country was concerned.

The greens of the trees contrasted with the white of the snow. As Clint rode, he could keep his eye on the same patch of rocks and watch as they slowly shifted color with the different angle of the sun. And the sun seemed to come from everywhere since the sky loomed overhead like a sheet that had been pulled over Clint's head.

Looking straight up could make a man dizzy or even give him the sense that he could fall off the face of the earth. When Clint snapped his reins and got Eclipse running at a full gallop, they both seemed to be racing the clouds themselves.

Wind wrapped around them and whistled in their ears.

The land stretched out forever and those mountains loomed like the giant, rocky backbone of the continent.

In the end, Clint rode toward those mountains for the sheer thrill of it. The moment he got close enough to smell the pine and feel the chill in the air, he knew it was worth every second.

In the back of his mind, he knew he'd backtracked a little, but that didn't matter too much. All that did matter was that he'd stocked up on supplies the day before and could go anywhere he pleased. Right now, the mountains pleased him more than he could express. Since he didn't have to express such things to Eclipse, he just flicked the reins and enjoyed the ride.

The day was spent with Clint working his way south while keeping those mountains in sight. He found a small town nestled in the shadow of those mountains and stopped there for a bite to eat. Most of the town was deserted, but the section that was still alive and kicking was doing some good business.

It turned out that it was the last spot for several days' ride for a man to get a hot meal and a relatively clean bed on his way to California or anywhere else farther west.

Folks there weren't too anxious to stick their noses in Clint's affairs, especially after seeing the gun strapped around his waist. Although Clint wasn't the sort to try and frighten anyone away, he didn't mind the peace and quiet continuing through his meal.

Since he hadn't even planned on sleeping with a roof over his head anytime soon, Clint put that town behind him and moved along while his food was still working its way through his belly. When he left that little dump of a town, Clint disappeared into the mountains for three days.

It was one of the most restful three days he'd had in some time.

Those days flowed by like a quick torrent of water, one right after the other, with Clint thinking about nothing but fishing for food and keeping his fire going. Eclipse had a chance to hone his climbing skills as he struggled up some of the steepest trails Clint could find. As far as he knew, he was the only one to find a few of those trails, and he hoped it was just as difficult for anyone else to find them if they passed that way as well. After all, Clint had benefited more than once from keeping a few secrets like those trails scattered throughout the country.

Clint spent the better part of one day scouting one of those secret trails to see just how far into the mountains it went. It was a winding path that was so narrow, he had to leave Eclipse tied to a tree before he could move on. He wasn't too surprised to discover that it wound up higher than he wanted to go on foot, so he headed back down and rode back to the spot he'd been using as a camp.

When he awoke the next morning, everything seemed to be going along just fine. That is, until he realized that he'd been robbed sometime during the night.

THIRTEEN

Clint searched the area several times over.

All he could find was a few scattered tracks and some broken twigs that pointed him to the northeast. It wasn't much to go on, especially since his saddlebags had been cleaned out and even the pockets of his jacket had been picked.

Standing in the middle of his camp, Clint looked around and tried to figure how that could have happened. He'd been dead tired the night before, but not so tired that he could have slept straight through while some bandits came by to pick him clean. The saddlebags had been close to where Eclipse was tethered and his jacket had been laid out under his bedroll.

Actually, the jacket had been under the end of his bedroll where his head had been resting. Not for the first time in the last few minutes, Clint looked around to see if he hadn't just accidentally dropped some of his things somewhere along the way.

But there was nothing to be found.

Only those tracks, the broken twigs, and a bunch of empty pockets were in that clearing with Clint and Eclipse.

And, not for the first time, Clint grumbled, "Son of a bitch."

Reflexively, Clint's hand went for his holster. The modified Colt was still there. It was a testament to whoever had robbed him that he'd even bothered to check. The weight of that gun at his side was as familiar to him as the weight of his arm hanging from his shoulder and would have been missed almost instantly.

Then again, if someone had asked him the day before, he would have figured the odds to be just as slight that some thief could sneak in and rob him blind.

Whoever had done this was good.

They were real good.

They were also the proud owners of nearly everything Clint owned, including all of his supplies. That last part was what bothered him the most. Money came and went. Possessions didn't last forever. But a man needed to eat and nature's bounty wasn't always enough to provide for him.

Since he didn't have much to gather, Clint was in the saddle and riding northeast in a matter of minutes. His stomach was growling and the more he dwelled on the fact that he didn't have any coffee, the more he wanted a cup.

By the time hunger really sank its teeth into him, Clint was glad that he hadn't gone too far from Mud Foot. He might have been meandering for the last several days, but Eclipse managed to get back to town after just over one day's ride.

In that amount of time, Clint was more aggravated than hungry. Since the bandits had taken his rifle as well as most everything else, he'd been forced to hunt with his pistol. The modified Colt was a hell of a side arm, but not much for bagging live game.

Rather than go through the hassle of getting within pistol range of a deer or rabbit, Clint lived off of berries until he made it back into town. The first stop he made when he got there was the first restaurant he could find. Although he'd been in that same place not too long ago, everyone there looked at him like he was a wild man who'd run in from the woods.

Of course, he did look the part.

"What . . . um . . . can I get for you?" the server asked as he did his best not to react to Clint's stench.

Digging into the bottom of his pocket, Clint pulled out some coins and slapped them onto the table. "Whatever I can get for this much," he said.

The server added up what he could see and shrugged. "Some stew and bread will be about all I can do."

"How about something cold to drink?" Clint asked. "It's been a hell of a day."

Laughing at that, the server walked away and came back with some lemonade. "Here you go. I'll be right back with the rest."

When Clint felt that lemonade trickle down his throat, he almost broke out laughing himself. His life wasn't exactly in danger, but it was nice to get something in his stomach without having to fight tooth and nail for it. The stew that was set in front of him actually made him feel human again. At the very least, it took the edge off the anger that had been rooting inside him since he'd first discovered what had happened.

As much as he wanted to take a bath and get a shave, Clint didn't think the barber would be willing to extend him much credit. Besides, he knew of one man in town who owed him at least a steak dinner. One thing was certain, Jebediah Cobbler could certainly afford it.

Jeb's promise to feed him all the steaks he could eat rattled in his brain. So did his offer to pay for Clint's supplies. While Clint never did take to accepting handouts, he figured he'd done enough favors for folks throughout the years to accept some jerked beef, coffee, and sugar.

As for replacing the rest of his things, Clint had a few ideas about that.

After wolfing down his food, Clint headed straight for the Georgia Peach. It was the middle of the day, so the saloon wasn't even half full. When he stepped through the door, Clint noticed every eye in the place fix on him and then turn away. Only one person regarded him as something more than a vagrant who'd wandered in to escape the elements.

"Clint?" Brooke asked as she walked around from behind the bar. "Is that you?"

"Yeah. It's me."

"What happened? Did you live with a pack of wolves for the last few days?"

"Where's Jeb?" he asked, ignoring the smirk that only grew on Brooke's face the closer she got.

That smirk dropped away as she shook her head. "I don't know where he is. Nobody does."

FOURTEEN

"What do you mean nobody knows where he is?" Clint asked.

"He left after he lost his house and nobody's seen him since."

Clint took hold of Brooke by the shoulders and looked straight into her eyes. "I know it hasn't been that long, but I've been away for a while."

As politely as she could, Brooke shrugged out of Clint's grasp and took a step back. Her nose pinched up just a little and a scowl crept across her face. "Sorry, Clint, but if we're going to be this close together, you're going to need to take a bath."

The tub took up a good portion of Brooke's kitchen and looked more like an oversized barrel that had been sawed in half. Clint sat in there with his arms draped over the sides, savoring the last pot of hot water that Brooke had poured in. As he continued to scrub, Clint felt something cool trickle along his back. He jumped and reached back there to catch Brooke pouring something out of a small glass vial.

"It's just some lavender oil," she said. "No need to get all jumpy."

"Is that a hint to let me know a simple bath won't do the job?"

"Hint? Not really. I just don't like my men smelling like they were pulled out from under a rotten log."

Rubbing in the oil, Clint asked, "Am I clean enough for you to answer my question?"

"Oh. You mean about Jeb?"

"That's the one. Start with what happened after I left and go on from there."

Brooke pulled a stool up next to the tub and rolled up her sleeves. "I don't know all of it where Jeb's concerned, but I do know that he didn't buy his house like he said he was going to."

"Are you certain?"

She nodded. "There's a notice on his door saying it's for sale."

"All right. What happened to Jeb?"

"He left," she said with a shrug. "At least, that's what I hear. Someone who works at the livery came into the Peach and said Jeb cleared out his horse and wagon and left town."

"And nobody knows where he went?"

She shook her head and leaned forward to scrub Clint's shoulders.

"Doesn't that strike you as odd?"

After thinking about it for a few moments, Brooke shrugged. "Until you came along, I never said more than two words to the man. Folks pick up and leave all the time. New folks come through and some of them stay." Adding a little bite to her voice, she said, "That's how most towns work, you know."

"Sure, folks come and go, but Jeb seemed awfully intent on paying for that house. Plus, it just doesn't sit right that he would disappear after all the trouble he had with Abe and his brother. Have they gone missing as well?"

Brooke seemed distracted as she washed Clint's chest, but soon met his glance. "Do we really need to talk about this now?" she asked as her hands slipped below the water.

She wasn't the only one having trouble focusing on the topic of conversation. Now that he'd had some food and was cleaned off, Clint was becoming very aware of the effect Brooke's hands were having upon him. "Have you heard anything about Abe?" he forced himself to ask.

Chewing on her lower lip, Brooke made a show of thinking that over. She also eased her hands along the front of Clint's body until they slipped between his legs. And, just as quickly, she eased them back up again. "They're still in jail," she replied while standing up and drying her hands on a nearby towel.

"And before you ask if I'm certain," she added. "I am. Abe's mother stopped by to ask if anyone from the Peach would tell the sheriff that Abe truly was cheated and that he was justified in being angry at Jeb."

Clint couldn't help but smile when he heard that. "She doesn't know too much about how saloons operate, does she?"

"No," Brooke replied. "She doesn't. And I also don't think she wants to think that her son is an angry drunk who is better off in a cage. Either way, it wasn't Abe or his brother who made Jeb disappear. They don't even have enough folks around here who like them who would do such a thing if they were asked."

"And that answers the next question I was about to ask."

As Clint stood up, Brooke handed him a towel. She even slipped her hands around his waist to work the towel across the small of his back.

"I guess that means you'll just have to put all that out of your mind for a while," she whispered. "Now that you're all washed up, I'm more inclined to keep you around for myself."

"That reminds me. I might need to borrow a few dollars to buy some supplies."

"Didn't you take Jeb up on his offer before you left the last time?"

"I did, but . . . well . . . it's a long story."

Brooke smiled mischievously. "How come I'm getting the impression that I want to hear that story?"

Clint rolled his eyes and took the towel from her so he could finish drying off.

"Are you avoiding me, Clint Adams?" When Clint turned his back to her, she practically jumped around so she was in front of him again. "Now I know I want to hear about it!"

"It's nothing, really."

"I'll be the judge of that."

Clint let out a sigh and said, "Those supplies were stolen from my camp. They were stolen along with damn near everything else I had. Now are you happy?"

Lowering her head a bit and sticking out a pouting lip, Brooke said, "Aw, did someone some along and rob the big, bad Gunsmith?"

"You see? This is why I didn't want to say anything."

Still wearing a little smile, Brooke tugged at the ribbon that held the front of her dress shut. "Come on now," she purred. "I can think of a way to make you feel better."

FIFTEEN

This time, when she tilted that bottle of lavender oil, Brooke let it trickle down the front of her own body. The cool fluid ran down her neck, followed the contour of her torso, and finally dripped between her breasts. She was completely naked and kneeling on her bed. Clint was lying on his back, between her legs, and enjoying the view.

He kept his hands on her hips for as long as he could manage. When she started rubbing the oil into her skin, however, keeping his hands in that spot was awfully difficult.

Brooke tilted her head back and smiled at the way Clint tensed beneath her. She arched her back slightly and let out a slow breath as her hands slid over her nipples, leaving them hard and glistening with oil. She kept one hand on her breast while the other slid along the front of her body, tracing where the oil was going.

Keeping up their little game of leaving his hands where they were, Clint found himself gripping her tighter as he watched Brooke slowly ease her finger to the thatch of soft hair between her legs. Her hand was glistening with the scented oil, allowing her fingertip to ease right between the lips of her pussy.

As Brooke slid her finger in even more, she let out a low, satisfied moan.

Clint couldn't hold off any longer. His hands came away from her hips and reached up to cup her breasts. After keeping still for what felt like an eternity, that simple motion was enough to make him let out a contented moan himself.

"I was wondering what took you so long," she said. "I thought I might be losing my touch."

"You haven't lost anything," Clint said as he rolled her onto her side and positioned himself close to her.

Brooke draped one leg over Clint's side and ground her hips against him. It didn't take much for her to work him into a full erection. His skin was still a little wet from the bathwater, so their bodies slipped against each other as they embraced on the bed.

Wrapping his hands around her, Clint pulled Brooke in close while running a finger along the slope of her back. She knew exactly how to move to position herself just right. Once she was there, all Clint had to do was push his hips forward and he felt his cock slide into her.

The moment she felt him plunge all the way in, Brooke let out what sounded like a growl. With a burst of strength, she pushed Clint onto his back once more and climbed on top of him. This time, she pinned him in place while straddling him. Leaning down, she pressed her full breasts against Clint's stomach and slid them all the way up to his chest.

The combination of oil and water mixed perfectly this time, allowing her to slide along his skin with ease. Her legs slipped up and down along his side until she felt his hard penis touching the sweet spot between her legs.

Clint reached down to guide himself back inside her. He kept hold of her backside and pulled her close while thrusting his hips forward. Their bodies met, sending shivers down both of their spines. Brooke arched her back and closed her eyes while Clint began pumping his hips up into her.

Pressing her hands flat against his chest, she squirmed every now and then to make sure he got to the right spots inside her. When she did feel him enter her in just the right way, the muscles in her thighs clamped even tighter around him.

Brooke was already tight enough, but when her muscles started flexing, it almost drove Clint out of his mind. He grabbed onto her with both hands while pumping even harder into her. Soon, she was bucking and tossing her hair back and forth as he drove her into a frenzy. When his hand slipped along some oil that had been rubbed onto her backside, Clint accidentally gave her bottom a little smack.

Brooke's eyes snapped open and she let out a little yelp.

"You liked that, huh?" Clint asked.

"God, Clint, you are always full of surprises."

Clint gave her another little spank as he buried his cock deep inside her. He could feel her starting to tremble, and it wasn't long before her first climax rippled through her body.

"I'm not done with you yet," he said as he rolled her onto her back.

Brooke was out of breath and didn't have enough breath to say another word. Soon, what little breath she did manage to take was let out in a prolonged, satisfied moan.

SIXTEEN

As much as Clint enjoyed the game of poker, he never really considered playing it for a living. Fortunately for him, everyone else at the tables in the Georgia Peach was of the same frame of mind. Even more fortunate was the fact that Clint had more experience than most of the locals combined.

In the space of two nights, Clint had built up a small loan from Brooke into enough to get himself some supplies as well as some pocket money to replace what he'd lost when he was robbed. After handing back what he'd borrowed, Clint got a sad, pouting look from Brooke in return.

"Oh, come on now," he said. "Enough with the puppy-dog eyes."

Brooke dropped the act and slid her arms around him. "Does this mean you're going to leave?"

"Well, I wasn't planning on buying a house."

"Be serious, Clint. A girl doesn't exactly like to have money slapped into her hand seconds before a man leaves her."

"I've heard there are plenty of girls who live by that very thing."

She swatted his arm and started walking with him still in tow. "You know what I mean!"

"I've already stayed on longer than I thought. I appreciate the loan, but it's time for me to get going."

"Will you at least come with me to the bank so I can deposit this? Considering the trouble that's been going on around here, it's not a good idea to walk around carrying money without some protection."

Clint nodded. "You bet. And I'll even treat you to dinner before I go." When he saw the happy look on her face, Clint raised a finger and added, "But it's just dinner. Otherwise, I'll never be able to get myself to ride out of here."

Tilting her head a bit, Brooke asked, "You promise you'll come back before too long?"

Clint took her in his arms and planted a lingering kiss on her full, soft lips. When he eased back again, he could feel her melting against him. "I promise."

She did her best to regain her composure and did a fairly good job. "All right then. The bank's this way. I already know where I want to go for supper and I'm thinking of a couple different ways to tempt you into my favorite kind of dessert."

After the nights he'd spent with Brooke Abernathy, Clint didn't have it in him to try and resist her any longer. Both of them knew that if one of them came up with something good enough, he would be staying on for at least one more night. With those possibilities running through their minds, they headed down the street to the only bank in Mud Foot.

It was a small building that was constructed to look like a big brick with a few small windows cut in the sides. Like most good banks, this one resembled a jailhouse in that it looked capable of surviving a twister as well as a battering ram. The only difference was the one set of larger windows up front, decorated with frilly, sun-bleached curtains.

They got there without incident. In fact, the streets were particularly bare considering it was getting close to the end of the workday. Once inside, Clint and Brooke only had to wait behind a solitary farmer who was taking out a few dollars to buy supplies. Brooke stepped up to the teller's window and slapped down the money Clint had given her.

The man behind the thin iron bars had a wide face and plenty of color in his cheeks. A small mustache sprouted from beneath his bulbous nose. "Evening, Miss Abernathy," he said. "What can I do for you?"

"I'd like to put this in my account."

"Sure thing." Glancing at Clint, the teller asked, "Who's your friend?"

Without looking at him, she patted Clint's shoulder and replied, "He's my bodyguard. A girl can't be too careful these days."

The teller had already counted up the money and was scribbling on a slip of paper. "That's very true," he said without taking notice of the joking smirk on Brooke's face. "Especially after what happened to poor Mr. Cobbler."

Those words stuck like a cold knife in Clint's gut. In some way, he felt like he'd been expecting them all along. "What happened to him?" Clint asked as he stepped forward.

The teller was taken aback by Clint's sudden rush to his window and flinched at the intensity on Clint's face. "You . . . you didn't hear about it?"

"No," Clint replied as he tried to take away some of the edge from his voice. "Why don't you tell me?"

But the teller looked over to Brooke instead. "Surely you heard?"

She merely shrugged.

After Clint cleared his throat, he regained the teller's attention. "Enlighten us."

"It happened no more than a few paces from the front door of this very bank," the teller explained. "Mr. Cobbler was on his way over here and he was held up at gunpoint."

"When was this?" Clint asked.

"A few days ago. A little under a week or so. I thought everyone in town would have heard about it."

"Go on."

Now that he was on a familiar subject and Clint had backed off a step, the teller was speaking in a much more fluid voice. "The sheriff was in here after it happened to talk to me because I was working when it happened."

"Really? What did you see?"

"I was at the window, getting ready to close up. Every night, I need to make sure the curtains are drawn and the sign is turned. Anyway, I saw Mr. Cobbler crossing the street and waving for me to hold off on locking the door. At least, I guess that's what he wanted."

"Makes sense," Clint said without trying to sound too insistent. "Go on."

"Mr. Cobbler crossed the street and headed for the front door. Well, since the window is on this side of the door, I couldn't see him for a few seconds. I didn't lock up and waited for him to come on inside. When he didn't, I took a look out to see where he'd gone."

The teller leaned forward and lowered his voice, even though there wasn't anyone else in that part of the bank except for himself, Brooke, and Clint. "When I looked outside, I saw Mr. Cobbler talking to another fellow."

"Who was it?" Clint asked.

"He had his back to me and all I could see was his shoulder and an arm, but he seemed awfully mad at something."

"Even though he had his back to you?" Brooke asked.

"He was hunched forward and even pushing Mr. Cobbler," the teller said in an urgent whisper. "I think he might have had a gun, but I didn't see one for certain."

"Is this where Mr. Cobbler would come if he wanted to pay off what he owed on his house?" Clint asked.

The teller mulled that over for a second or two before nodding. "I believe he did get a loan through us."

"And what happened after you saw that other man pushing Jeb around?"

"He pushed Mr. Cobbler right into the alley, so I

couldn't see either of them anymore. There was some scuffling and I think there was even a fight."

With even more skepticism in her voice, Brooke asked, "You know that even though you couldn't see either of them?"

Shrugging, the teller replied, "I went into the manager's office to take a look out his window. I couldn't see much, but I heard scuffling. I even heard what had to be someone being pushed right against this building."

Clint nodded. "And I suppose you told all this to the sheriff?"

"Of course I did. But he hasn't found anything. At least, he hasn't told me about any new clues or the like."

"And you haven't heard from Jeb?"

The teller shook his head. "No, sir. I don't think anyone has."

"I knew that much," Brooke said.

"What about the loan on his house?" Clint asked.

Lowering his eyes, the teller winced a bit when he said, "if we don't get a payment soon, the bank will have to claim that house. I heard the manager talking about that earlier today. He was quite . . . agitated. It's been months since Mr. Cobbler has made a payment."

With that, the teller accepted Brooke's deposit and placed his hands on the counter. "Is there anything else I can do for you folks?"

"No," Clint said. "You've been real helpful."

Brooke needed to hurry to catch up to Clint, but managed to do so before he got too far out of the bank. She even managed to circle around and get in front of him. "Where are you off to?" she asked breathlessly.

"I'm looking for the sheriff's office."

"Then you're going the wrong way."

SEVENTEEN

"Well," Clint grumbled as he stood at the bar inside the Georgia Peach, "that wasn't very helpful."

It had been less than twenty minutes since he and Brooke had left the bank. Half of that time was spent getting to the sheriff's office and waiting for the lawman to notice they were there. It took a few minutes for Clint to convince the sheriff to tell him anything and the same amount of time for Clint to realize that he was better off questioning the bank teller.

Now that they were back in the Peach, Clint suddenly found himself looking down at a mug of beer.

"Here you go," Brooke said. "Just as I promised."

"When was that?"

"While you were sulking on the walk back here. Now drink up. Looks to me like you could use it."

The brew went a long way in taking the scowl off Clint's face. Seeing Brooke smiling at him the way she did was enough to finish the job. "What are you so happy about?" he asked. "It seems to me like we didn't get a damn thing accomplished."

"I'm just amazed that you could win so much money in poker."

"Huh?" Clint asked.

"I can practically hear every last thing that's running through your head. Aren't gamblers supposed to have faces like brick walls?"

"All right then," he said while looking her straight in the eyes. "Tell me what I'm thinking."

Brooke pressed her fingertips to her forehead and put on a look of dramatic concentration. "You're thinking, 'To hell with that sheriff.' "

"You don't get a prize for that one. I actually said that after we walked out of his office."

She held up her hand to silence him. "Also . . . you're thinking that you want to try and find out what happened to Jeb Cobbler on your own."

"Anything else?"

"Oh, yes," she said while taking her hands away from her temple and giving Clint a wink. "But I shouldn't say such things in public places."

"All right, so maybe you do have a talent."

"Why would you be so concerned about Jeb? Did you even know him before that game?"

"No, but that's not the point. It seems obvious that something's happened to him and nobody seems to care. That's the point."

"It's not that nobody cares," Brooke said. "It's just that . . ." As she trailed off, her eyes drifted to a spot over Clint's shoulder. When she still couldn't think of anything to say, she shifted her gaze back to him. "Folks come and go, that's all."

"Yeah and it seems like Jeb's the one who's gone."

"You don't even know that anything bad happened to him. Maybe he just decided to pack up and leave. It's not like he was having much luck around here."

Clint shook his head. "He was happy about paying off for that house. I could see that much for certain. You were there."

"I was." After being scrutinized by Clint for a few more seconds, she added, "He was excited about that house. I admit that much. So what?"

"So, I intend on seeing if there's anything worth fussing about as far as Jeb Cobbler is concerned."

Clint downed the rest of his beer and headed for the door.

"Where are you going?" Brooke called out after him.

"I want to check on the spot where Jeb was last seen."

By now, Brooke had already come to his side and was reaching for the door. "Then I'll come with you."

"No," Clint replied as he took hold of her and prevented her from walking past him. "You need to stay here."

"But I feel bad about all this. I'd really like to help."

"And you can be a big help if you stay here and see if you can find out anything where Jeb's concerned."

"Stay here? But I told you he hasn't been here for a while."

"That's what you've seen," Clint pointed out. "I'm more interested in what you can hear. Ask around about Jeb while you're working tonight. Most of the rumors flowing through any town go through the saloon and this is the best place around here. I'll bet you can find out plenty if you just make it your job to ask."

She nodded slowly at first, but then built up a head of steam. "You're right! There's so much gossip going around between these drunks that I tend to block most of it out."

"Start listening to it and we should be in business," Clint said as he opened the front door. "I'll check in with you later tonight."

EIGHTEEN

Clint retraced his steps to the bank. He stayed on the other side of the street until he passed the brick building, and then crossed when he was a few doors away from it. Doing his best to stick close to the storefronts without drawing attention, he made it to the alley and quickly ducked into the shade.

Although the teller had been a lot of help, it was also plain to see that he watched every little thing that went on outside his window. Considering how much he'd told and how quickly he'd told it, there had to have been a whole lot more that the teller would have said to someone he knew better. Clint just wanted to remain off that list if possible.

He kept his steps quiet and was careful not to knock anything over as he worked his way down the alley. Even if the teller did keep his mouth shut, Clint didn't want the other man buzzing around him like a gnat when he was trying to focus on the smallest possible detail.

The first thing that became clear was the fact that not many people walked down that alley. Although there were plenty of tracks in the dirt close to the bank's side door, those were several yards in. At the alley's opening, there were a few random steps, but only one set of tracks that caught Clint's eye.

Those tracks were barely visible, but belonged to two men and were in the basic vicinity of where the teller had spotted Jeb and the second man. Those tracks didn't tell Clint much of anything, but they did mark a spot for him to start his search.

Taking advantage of the angle of the sunlight, which cast a few beams into the alley, Clint got down on one knee and took a closer look. He managed to see a few scrapes in the wall that were just new enough to match the teller's story.

It didn't take much of a detective to tell that there'd been a scuffle in that spot not too long ago. After finding those first few scrapes, Clint was able to pick out several more that had to have been made by something being slammed against that wall or even dragged against it. It could have been a belt buckle, the handle of a gun, or any number of things. What mattered was that whoever had scraped up that wall hadn't done so by doing the two-step.

Clint followed those scrapes a little further into the alley to a spot where they narrowed down to a smaller spot. Although there were fewer of them, the ones he could see were a whole lot deeper. Leaning in closer to the wall, Clint was even able to make out a more definable shape. These weren't just scrapes. These were more like gouges and they were most definitely at a man's waist level. Clint nodded as he stood up, imagining one of those men being slammed against the wall so hard that his belt buckle would leave a mark.

With that thought in mind, Clint shifted his glance upward until he was staring straight ahead. Sure enough, a belt buckle hadn't been the only thing to get bashed against that wall. The dark smears on the brick had been washed off by one of the bank workers or a recent rain, but the stain was still easy enough to see.

It was a warm enough summer for the smear to have attracted more than just Clint's attention. Ants and flies were circling those stains, telling Clint that they weren't made of red paint. He touched his finger to the wall just to be certain and knew almost immediately that it was blood.

Now that he'd been standing there for a little while, he could pick up the smell of the blood as well. Clint looked around the alley for anything else that could be of help. Although there was plenty to swipe up in there, he didn't have any way of telling what boards had been broken by a fight or what bottles had been tossed in by a passing drunk.

For all he knew, all of that stuff could have been dropped during Jeb Cobbler's last moments in Mud Foot. It was just as possible that none of it had anything to do with Jeb. Just to be certain, Clint started at the back of that alley and worked his way up to the front. All he got for his troubles was a few questioning glances from folks passing by on the street.

Since Clint could feel the curious teller approaching one of the windows, he left the alley and walked down the street. Sure enough, he spotted the man inside the bank staring out at him the way a kid stared at fireflies trapped in a jar.

Clint tossed a wave toward the bank and kept walking. There was someone else he wanted to see.

NINETEEN

It was just past suppertime when Clint made his way back to the Georgia Peach. He came through the doors with a spring in his step and a smile on his face that Brooke was very surprised to see. She met him at the bar and placed her hands upon her hips.

"Well, don't you look like the cat that swallowed the canary?" she said. "Did you find your friend?"

"Nope," Clint said. "But I did find out that there was most definitely a brawl in the alley next to the bank."

Brooke waited for a few seconds before her smile started to fade. "Maybe I don't want to know why that makes you so happy."

Shaking his head, Clint led her to one of the nearby tables. "I'm not happy about the fight. I'm happy that I think I know what happened to Jeb."

"Really? What happened?"

"Well, I didn't find out all the details, but I'm pretty sure he was fighting with Melvin Grimley in that alley."

"How do you know that?"

"Because that just makes sense since Melvin seemed ready to take a shot at him and me at that card game. I asked about him at some of the other places in town where cards are dealt and nobody's seen him since Jeb disappeared."

One of the other girls working at the Peach brought Clint his normal mug of beer and he took a quick drink.

"Seems like he sat in on a few games," Clint continued, "but only lost them all and kicked up a stink. Right about the time when Jeb was at the bank, Melvin stormed out and hasn't been heard from since. The only thing is that I couldn't find anyone who had the vaguest notion of where Melvin went."

Suddenly, Brooke's eyes snapped open wide and she grabbed hold of Clint's wrist. "Oh, I heard something about that!" she said excitedly.

"About Melvin?"

She nodded so quickly that her curled hair dropped down to nearly cover her face. Brushing the hair behind her ear, she said, "I was asking about Jeb just like you asked me to and it just so happened that one of the fellows drinking here played cards with Melvin every week. He played with him not too long ago, in fact, and said that Melvin was cross about something."

"Did he know what he was cross about?"

Brooke cocked her head a bit and said, "You should know better than that, Clint. When you men get together, you barely remember to introduce yourselves. I swear you'd ignore it if someone's hair was on fire if it meant you could continue your game."

"Not everyone is like that, you know."

After getting a stern glare from Brooke, Clint shrugged and added, "Well, almost everyone maybe."

She nodded and continued now that Clint had said the right thing. "The fellow I talked to did recall Melvin going on about Farewell Mountain."

"Farewell Mountain?" Clint said under his breath. Although the name sounded familiar, he couldn't put his finger on it right away. Suddenly, it snapped into focus. "I remember now," he said with a snap of his fingers. "That was the name of the place where Melvin had that deed he put up to cover the last bet of our game."

"Sounds about right. He was pretty upset about losing it and went on about how he was going to get it back since he never should have lost it in the first place."

"Is it supposed to be some kind of deed that's been panning out?" Clint asked.

In response to that, Brooke merely shrugged. "A mine, a claim, some bit of land, I don't really know. All I know is that this fellow said that Melvin was awfully cross about losing that deed. Or was it a claim?" She shook her head and waved off her own question. "Whichever it was, he wants it back. This fellow who was talking to me said that Melvin probably went off to get it back."

"Is that a fact?"

She nodded. "That's what he told me."

"Is this fellow still around?"

Brooke craned her neck to get a look around the place. Although the Georgia Peach wasn't full to brimming, there were enough people in there to make up a good-sized crowd. After studying the faces she could see, she looked back at Clint and shook her head. "I don't see him."

Taking another sip of his beer, Clint let out a long breath. "You did a real good job. See how much you can learn by doing a little bit of digging?"

"I was really surprised. Maybe folks are paying more attention than I thought they were."

The possibility that Brooke was the oblivious one crossed Clint's mind, but he kept it there rather than say anything out loud. What mattered was that that situation seemed to have changed for the better.

"Any idea why they call it Farewell Mountain?" he asked.

"Some say it's cursed. Others say there's bandits or

wild Indians that live up there. Mostly, anyone who heads for that mountain," Brooke explained while holding up one hand to wave, "says farewell to the rest of the world before they drop off of it."

"People have disappeared?"

"Oh, yes. Plenty of them. The last anyone sees them is when they set off from here or some other place where they get supplies. There's even talk of a railroad line that was meant to go through there, but got swallowed up and was abandoned."

"Now, that's a bit harder to swallow," Clint said.

"Say what you like, those are the rumors and that's why it's called Farewell Mountain."

"Fair enough. Now, the next thing I need to know is how to get there."

TWENTY

It was early the next morning when Clint once again left Mud Foot. His saddlebags weren't as heavy as normal, but he had enough supplies to carry him through. He also had a destination in mind, even though it was supposed to be cursed.

He smiled when he thought about that word. Whenever more than a few bad things happened in any given place, it was supposed to be cursed. If half of the cursed places in the country had truly earned that name, the world would have already been overrun by devils several times over. Even so, Clint wasn't about to just ride straight up that mountain like he owned it. He knew for a fact that there was at least one band of thieves sneaking around. If he was lucky, he would catch up to them as well.

According to Brooke, there was only one trail that led to Farewell Mountain. Since that was most likely the trail Jeb or Melvin would have used, Clint didn't bother trying to find another one. Instead, he rode out of town and headed straight into the local haunting grounds. It didn't take long for him to see why someone would think that the area was better left alone. Hardly any sunlight trickled through the thick canopy of leaves covering the trail. In fact, the narrow path seemed more like a tunnel as it twisted and turned its way between thick, gnarled foliage.

Trees leaned in from all sides and roots reached up from the dirt. Already, Clint could see how more than a few unwary travelers could meet their end before they even got within sight of the mountain. Any horse that was moving too quickly would surely be tripped up by some of those roots and break its neck. Anyone in the saddle when that happened would either be crushed or too broken to crawl out of the tangled mess of bushes.

Trying to pick up any sort of tracks was less than futile. Dents in the uneven ground could look like wheel ruts or they could have been left behind by a fat snake. Any useful tracks would have been wiped away by the swaying bushes or erased by the winds that tore through the enclosed space every couple of seconds.

At times, Clint wondered if he'd gotten himself turned around or sidetracked onto a different trail altogether. More often than not, he couldn't even see the mountain. Most of the time, he couldn't see any mountains whatsoever. But since there were no places where the trail branched off, he figured he would just keep forging ahead until he found a reason to do otherwise.

That reason came even sooner than he'd expected.

"There he goes!" a voice shouted from off the trail to Clint's left.

Pulling back on the reins, Clint brought Eclipse to a stop and stared in that direction. He kept perfectly still so he could try to make out any sight or sound that might tell him what was going on.

Although he could hear the rustling of leaves and the scampering of several sets of feet, he couldn't see much of anything through the dense layers of branches. If anyone was aware he was there, they sure weren't concerned enough to lower their voices.

"I see him!"

"Cut off the trail to the left! I'll take the right!"

When Clint heard a gunshot crack through the air, he jumped down from his saddle and looped Eclipse's reins around the top of the closest bush. When the Darley Arabian felt that little bit of resistance, he knew to stay put and wait for Clint to come get him.

Clint hunched down low and picked a quick path through the bushes. Whatever noise he made while doing so was easily canceled out by the shouting voices and increasing amount of gunfire.

Once Clint had struggled ten to fifteen paces off the trail, some of those gunshots sent rounds that hissed close enough to Clint's head to make him stop and duck even lower. It was still impossible for him to see more than a tangle of green and brown, shot through with a few stray beams of sunlight. When the figure exploded from the bushes no more than two feet in front of him, Clint drew the Colt out of pure reflex.

Fortunately, the man that had just appeared from the trees seemed just as surprised to see Clint. His eyes were wide and his face was covered by too many scratches to count. His hands were wrapped around a Sharps rifle.

"It's you," the man grunted.

Clint didn't know who the hell the man was, and didn't get a chance to ask for a name before he saw the butt of that rifle come swinging toward his head. Although he was off balance, Clint did manage to lean back to avoid the rifle before it broke his jaw.

"I found another one!" the man shouted as he shifted the rifle in his hands to take a shot at Clint.

Still stumbling backward, Clint did his best to aim at the hip and pull his trigger before that rifle blew his head from his shoulders. Two shots blasted through the air so close together that Clint didn't even know if his was first or second.

Hot lead whipped through the air so close to his head

that Clint swore he could feel a breeze. He allowed himself to drop to the ground just to be out of the way if that rifle went off again. Apparently, the rifleman had had the same idea since he'd disappeared once more into the bushes. Either that, or he'd been hit and was stretched out on the ground.

"Goddammit, I said get the hell over here! This one's got a gun!"

At least that answered that question.

Now that he knew the rifleman was still alive and kicking, Clint had to decide what to do about it. His head was still spinning from the sudden burst of commotion and his blood was slamming through his veins. After taking a few deep breaths, he could think clearly enough to come up with a plan.

Pushing himself backward using both legs, the rifleman didn't bother flopping over onto his belly until he'd put plenty of space between himself and the spot where he'd found Clint. After getting his legs beneath him, he hoisted himself up and spun around to face the sound of approaching footsteps.

A man with long, stringy hair held a sawed-off shotgun in his right hand and a machete in his left. His face was covered with a bandanna, but the shock in his eyes was plain enough to see. "Ease up, Lou. It's me."

Although he recognized the other one, Lou wasn't about to let down his guard. Instead, he scrambled around to get a look at the bushes in front of him while aiming the Sharps at anything that moved. "There's another one out here."

"You sure about that?"

"Hell, yes, I'm sure! He took a shot at me!"

The eyes shifted over that bandanna as the man with the shotgun took a closer look at the bushes where Lou had been. "You swing around behind me," he said as he pointed ahead and to his left. "I'll see if I can find this other fellow."

Rather than pay any mind to what the shotgunner said, Lou obeyed the hand signals he'd been given. Rather than go back while the shotgunner went forward, both men split up to flank the spot where Clint had been spotted.

After taking a few steps, both men practically disappeared into the foliage. In a matter of seconds, they'd worked their way up to spot some movement not far from where Lou had come from. Neither man said a word or made a sound as they crept up on their target.

Lou spotted the shotgunner just in time to see three fingers get held up. As the shotgunner counted down, Lou readied himself to launch a little surprise attack of his own.

TWENTY-ONE

Lou crawled on his belly through the bushes while more gunshots and trampling footsteps echoed behind him. Although he didn't know who Clint was, he wasn't in the habit of letting just anyone take a shot at him and get away with it. Besides, it seemed that he was going to be able to get nice and close before anyone knew he was there.

When the shotgunner was through with his countdown, he signaled for both of them to charge forward. They exploded from the bushes with guns drawn and came face-to-face with the source of the rustling that had drawn them to that spot.

Looking back at both men, Eclipse blinked a few times and looked away.

"I swear, Jack," Lou said. "There was someone else here and he took a shot at me."

"It's probably the same asshole we were chasing and you let us get drawn away so he could move on."

"No, it was—"

"Just work your way back that way," Jack said, doing his best to point back into the bushes and not point his shotgun at Lou's head. "And pray to Christ that you didn't let that son of a bitch get away!"

With that, Jack turned and disappeared into the bushes amid a few rustling footsteps. That left Lou there with his Sharps in hand and an angry scowl on his face. Choking back his rage, he turned his back to the Darley Arabian and prepared to crawl through some more bushes.

Lou made it less than three steps before he felt the touch of iron against his right temple.

"That's far enough," Clint whispered.

When Lou turned to get a look at who was speaking, Clint tapped the Colt against his head once more.

"Just drop the rifle and put your face to the dirt."

Gnashing his teeth together, Lou did as he was told and stretched himself out so he was lying flat on the ground. Only after he'd laid his head down did he see Clint emerge from where he'd been hiding.

Hunkered down to less than half his height, Clint shuffled out from behind a particularly thick clump of bushes. Even after the little bit of moving he'd done through the branches, his face was almost as cut up as Lou's. He kept the Colt pressed against Lou's head as he reached out to take the Sharps.

"How many of you are there?" Clint asked.

"Go fu—"

"I wouldn't finish that sentence," Clint said as he leaned down on the Colt hard enough to force Lou's mouth into the dirt. "That is, unless you were going to finish that off with an accurate count."

After a few seconds, the pressure eased up and Lou was able to lift his face enough to speak. "There's plenty of us to hunt down the likes of you. And if you're here to meet that asshole friend of yours, we'll hunt him down too."

"I still don't have an accurate count."

"Seven," Lou spit. "There's seven of us altogether."

Since he was holding Lou's head down with the Colt, Clint kept his eyes on the surrounding area. He could feel the slightest movement Lou made through the gun he held to his head. "And what's the name of this other man you're after?"

"You don't know?"

"I've got a bunch of friends," Clint said as his eyes focused upon a set of figures picking their way through the bushes. "One is named Jebediah and the other is named Melvin. You talking about either one of those?"

"Yeah. Maybe."

"Which one?"

"He's right here!" Lou suddenly screamed. Although he couldn't see much of anything from his spot on the ground, he'd been able to hear plenty since his ear was right against the earth.

The steps that had been moving away from Clint now stomped straight for him. There were also a few others converging on his as well. Although he could only see a small portion of Lou's face, Clint had no trouble telling that the other man was smiling.

As much as he wanted to shut Lou's mouth for good, Clint merely shoved the rifleman's face into the dirt as he got moving. He launched himself face-first into the bushes because he didn't have the time to be more careful. From what he could tell, the others would be able to see him at any moment.

To his left, Clint saw the bigger man who'd met up with Lou a few minutes ago. The man was still wearing his bandanna and he was still gripping his shotgun. As soon as Clint saw that shotgun bearing down on him, Clint extended both hands and dove for the next clump of bushes.

Fire and hot lead exploded behind him, sending broken branches and bits of leaves through the air. Clint's hands touched the ground as he curled himself into a ball. It wasn't until he'd stopped rolling that Clint was even certain he hadn't been hit.

Although every inch of him was either bruised or scraped, he hadn't caught any lead. The only way to keep that good fortune rolling was to keep moving. Even though he heard voices coming from somewhere ahead, Clint kept up his frantic pace and rushed ahead.

From the corner of his eye, Clint spotted something stretching out toward him that wasn't a branch. He instinctively shifted away from it and brought his Colt to aim in that direction. Just then, the branches Clint had been using for cover thinned out and exposed a small clearing no bigger than a large tabletop.

The arms reaching out for him were still coming and one of them managed to snag hold of Clint's shirt.

"I got him!" the big man who'd grabbed Clint hollered. Not only was this man bigger than Clint, but he seemed almost as big as some of the trees surrounding him. His wide face was covered in a beard and his bushy hair was held back by a bandanna tied around his head.

Just as Clint realized he was no longer moving, he felt his entire body get lifted off the ground. Two hands had clamped around his shoulders and were now picking him up like a rag doll. Although he couldn't move his gun arm more than an inch or so, Clint bent his wrist and pulled his trigger.

The Colt barked once and punched a hole into the dirt less than an inch from the giant's boot. That caused the big man to drop Clint like a hot rock and let out an angry snarl. With his lips curled back, the giant turned on Clint.

Locking eyes with the giant, Clint could feel the anger pouring off him like a heat wave. Just to stoke the fire a bit, he gave the giant a quick wink. Sure enough, that caused the big man to charge forward while letting out a feral snarl.

At the last moment, Clint stepped to the right and slammed his left fist deep into the giant's stomach. Knowing better than to end it there, he followed up with a swift knee into that same spot. Although that didn't drop the giant completely, it did double him over and take some of the steam from his stride.

Clint turned his back to the giant and picked the spot where he was going to run next. Before he could take another step, however, his way was blocked by a pair of men. One of them held a rifle and the other was the shotgunner with the bandanna over his face.

"Enough of this shit," the shotgunner said to Clint. "Hand over that gun and anything else you got or we'll bury you right where you stand."

TWENTY-TWO

Every time he took a breath, Clint could feel the noose cinching in tighter around his neck. Every second he let pass, the gunmen surrounding him got better situated in their positions. And by the sound of it, there were more gunmen on their way.

Before the shotgunner could get out one more threat, Clint snapped his arm up and took quick aim with the modified Colt. The gun spit out two rounds in quick succession before either of the two men in front of him knew what was happening.

The shotgunner was the first to drop and the man next to him was close on his heels. Both of them caught bullets in the arm or shoulder, which knocked them back quicker than a kick from a mule.

With those two shots still echoing through the air, Clint turned on his heels to see what the giant was doing. The big man was already barreling in on him. This time, he was swinging a machete similar to the one the shotgunner carried. Either the giant wasn't afraid of the Colt or he was too angry to notice it. Either way, he charged at Clint without anything else on his mind besides cutting him in two.

Clint did manage to pull his trigger, but it wasn't until

the giant had swung his machete toward his ribs. Staggering back as the Colt went off, Clint barely managed to clear a path for the machete before it cleared a path through him. The blade sliced through the air and Clint landed roughly on the ground.

With a wild look in his eyes, the giant grabbed the machete with both hands and glared at Clint. He then lifted the blade over his head, let out an inhuman growl, and ran forward.

Clint knew damn well that he couldn't dodge that blade forever. He also knew he couldn't survive a hit from the weapon when it was being swung by a monster like that. All of that flashed through his mind in the blink of an eye. In the next moment, his finger was tightening around his trigger.

The Colt barked again and again as it sent round after round into the giant's hulking body. Blood popped out in spots on his chest and stomach, but the giant still kept coming. His eyes were glazed over and his knuckles had turned white from holding on to the machete.

Clint's last shot drilled through the giant's forehead, snapping the big man's head back and causing him to lower his arms.

For a moment, Clint wasn't sure if the giant was going to give up the ghost or not. Finally, after letting out a shuddering grunt, the giant let go of the machete and keeled over. Clint was gone before the big man's back hit the dirt.

"Someone get after that son of a bitch!" the shotgunner shouted as he clamped a hand over the wound in his shoulder.

Lou and one of the others in his group ran into the small clearing with pistols in hand. They looked around frantically for a target, and turned pale the moment their eyes landed on the body of the big man with the machete.

"Holy shit," Lou said. "Is that Joey?"

The shotgunner grunted as he pulled himself to his feet and shifted his weapon to his other hand. "Yeah, it's Joey. That stranger gunned him down."

But Lou and the other gunman couldn't get their eyes off the giant's body. When they finally looked up again, they examined the surrounding woods as if they were haunted.

"What the hell are you two waiting for?" the shotgunner snarled.

"I didn't even think anyone could hurt Joey," the man next to Lou said.

"You want to let that stranger get away with it, then you just keep flapping your lips," the shotgunner said. "Otherwise, we can round him up and nail him to one of these goddamn trees!"

Still keeping one hand against his wound, the shotgunner glared at the others gathered around him.

"MOVE!"

Hearing that, all but one of the gunmen scattered like pheasants that had been flushed from a bush. A few of them had only just gotten to the clearing when they were shoved back out again by the shotgunner's bellowing voice. By the looks on their faces, they were more than happy to leave rather than stay and deal with the armed, wounded man.

Lou was the one who stayed behind, and he did so as if he hadn't even heard the shotgunner's threats. "You know who that fella was, Jack?"

Only now did the shotgunner let out a pained grunt as he walked over to a thick tree trunk. One more grunt, and Jack propped himself against the tree so he could examine his wound. "I didn't get much of a look at him."

"I did. He was that fellow we robbed on the trail southwest of town."

Jack furrowed his brow and then finally took another look at Lou. "The one who was asleep on top of all them supplies?"

"That's the one."

"Has Chris seen him yet?"

Lou shrugged. "I don't know. Chris and a few of the others were searching in the opposite direction. I don't even know if they came all the way back or not."

"They damn well better have come back!" Jack fumed. "If they didn't, they intended on leaving the rest of us to fight this asshole off on our own."

Although he cringed, Lou said, "They probably thought we'd be fine with Joey along with us."

"Yeah, you're right about that." Peeling back some bloody strips of sleeve that were sticking to his wound, Jack clenched his teeth and let out a hiss. "If that asshole was after some payback, I'd say he got it. Let's just try to get who we were after and get the hell out of here."

"I like the sound of that. I told you this damn mountain was cursed."

"Yeah," Jack grunted. "I guess we're gonna find that out the hard way."

TWENTY-THREE

Compared to the hell that was unleashed a few moments ago, the noise Clint made as he left that clearing was next to nothing. He kept his head down and his Colt ready while winding his way through the trees and bushes. Before too long, the foliage began to thin out again and he was able to pick up his pace.

Behind him, the rest of those gunmen were stomping around and shouting their threats in every direction. But despite all the tough talk and chest-thumping, Clint knew they were all scared. One of the oldest tricks to survive being outnumbered had once again shown its worth.

All a man had to do was take on the biggest member of the bunch to make all the others think twice. It was a trick that had the possibility to backfire in a major way, but when it worked, it could save that man's life. This time it had worked, but Clint wasn't anxious to push his luck.

The ground beneath Clint's boots began to slope to the right. It was a gradual slope, but Clint followed it all the same. Soon, he found himself jogging down an incline, and then he had to fight to keep from sliding. The incline dropped off quickly and emptied into a ditch that was at least four feet deep.

Not exactly a life-threatening fall, but it could present some big problems for someone who'd been moving too fast when they found it. By the looks of it, the woman at the bottom of the ditch just then could attest to that fact.

She was dressed in buckskins and weathered boots. Her jacket was buckled tight around her for added protection and her hat was hanging by its string around her neck. When she saw Clint, she immediately brought her gun up and aimed it with an unsteady hand.

One quick shift of his own arm allowed Clint to return the favor with his Colt.

"Are you one of them?" she asked.

Clint's eyes narrowed as he picked up on the fear in her eyes. "If I was," he told her, "you'd be dead already."

She took a moment to think that over before lowering her gun and letting out a pained groan. "If you're not going to shoot me, do you think you could give me a hand?"

The Colt stayed in Clint's hand as he worked his way down to the woman. Although the barrel of his gun didn't aim directly at her, it wouldn't take much more than a thought for him to correct that.

"You don't need the pist—" she started to say, but was cut off by a quick gesture from Clint.

He moved in closer to her and leaned so that his side was barely touching hers. That way, she could hear him just fine when he spoke to her in something just below a whisper. "There are plenty of armed men hereabouts," he said.

She started to respond, but stopped so she could lower her voice to match Clint's tone. "I know. I was trying to get away from them when I slipped and fell into this ditch."

"Are you hurt bad?"

"I don't think so," she replied while squirming a bit.

Although she merely pulled her leg to a better angle and shifted her back against the ground, the noise she made seemed like a log being dragged over a bed of dry leaves.

"Feels like I twisted my knee," she said. "My back hurts too, but that's just where I landed."

"Can you walk?"

"Yes," she said right away. "At least, I should be able to manage after you help me get to my feet. Right now, that seems to be the tricky part."

"All right then. For now, we'll just sit tight until those armed men I told you about decide to move on."

"And what if they don't?" she asked insistently.

"Then we have a better chance of taking them from here instead of when I'm dragging you out of this ditch or trying to help you along."

Reluctantly, she nodded. When she brought up her hand, it was wrapped around a Smith & Wesson pistol. The gun was a somewhat older model, but it was well maintained. When she raised it to aim at the top of the ditch, her hand was steady.

Clint nestled himself against the ground beside her. Despite the circumstances, he couldn't help but admire the feel of her body against him and the confidence with which she carried herself. Still, there were more questions running through his head than he could answer just then and that always made Clint a little nervous.

Suddenly, some footsteps drew closer to them. They came from the same direction that Clint had approached the ditch from, and were cautious enough to make Clint tense his finger upon his trigger. "Steady," he whispered. "Don't shoot unless you need to."

He could feel the woman pull in a nervous breath and nod. She still kept the gun in front of her, but lowered it so they could blend in a little better in their surroundings. As she got herself settled, Clint used his free hand to scrape at the edges of the ditch and pull down all the loose dirt he could reach.

Once she realized what Clint was doing, the woman used her free hand to join in. In a matter of seconds, they'd covered themselves with a thin layer of dirt. Since the nearby bushes were shaking with the approaching visitor, there wasn't time for them to do any more.

The seconds dragged by as if each one was weighted down. The longer he waited lying there in that ditch, the more vulnerable Clint felt. By the time the man stepped out of the trees and looked around, Clint was certain he and the woman were going to be gunned down in that spot.

When he saw the second armed man step out from behind the first, Clint felt like he was lying in a freshly dug grave. To make matters worse, he'd already started the job of filling in the hole.

TWENTY-FOUR

The two men approaching the ditch were definitely part of the group that had been chasing Clint. Although there wasn't much doubt in Clint's mind to begin with, he recognized one of the men's faces when the fellow stepped a little closer. At least this time Clint wasn't running or fighting, so he could get a better look at them.

Both men were carrying rifles and they also had gun belts strapped around their waists. They carried the rifles like they were more favored weapons than the pistols, which made sense since every member of this group seemed to have one.

They stood their ground and looked at the bushes in front of them. For the moment, they were a few paces away from the spot where the incline dropped off. The man in front crouched down a bit while the other one kept his rifle at his shoulder and ready to fire.

"You see anything, Randy?" the man in the back asked.

Randy was a younger fellow with light brown hair. His mustache covered his entire upper lip and drooped straight down into a goatee that was trimmed into a point just below his chin. Overall, the facial hair made him look about nineteen rather than seventeen.

"I know one of them came this way," Randy said.

"What about Chris?"

"I don't see either one."

As the two had been talking, Clint had managed to get his hand on a rock that was just big enough to fit in his fist. Bending that hand back as far as he could, he lifted his arm a bit and snapped his wrist forward to send the rock through the air.

It snapped a few thinner branches before landing with a thump in the bushes. Both gunmen snapped their eyes in that direction and readied their guns.

Without a word, Randy signaled for his partner to circle around to the left of where the sound had come from. After the other man crouched down and disappeared into the foliage, Randy remained kneeling in his spot as though he was in the front ranks of a firing line.

Clint could feel the woman tensing. He squeezed her shoulder to comfort her, but that was mainly to keep her from pulling her trigger out of sheer nerves. Even though he could see her lower her Smith & Wesson a bit, Clint found himself lifting his Colt.

Randy stayed put with his eyes narrowed and his rifle at the ready. He sighted along its barrel and intently watched the area where the noise had come from. In the minute that Clint watched, he didn't even see Randy blink.

Finally, Randy got into a low crouch and started moving toward the bushes where Clint had tossed the rock.

The woman's breaths were coming faster and faster. Her hands started to tremble and heat poured off her body.

When he'd first found that ditch, Clint felt as if he could break his neck if he'd fallen that far down. Now, it seemed as though he was lying in a half-dug trench with nothing but a few scoops of dirt and good fortune to keep him from being spotted.

He knew he could have shot both of those riflemen when they were in his sights, but there was no telling what

kind of trouble that would have unleashed. Clint wasn't
certain where the others had gone or if reinforcements had
arrived. All of those things were good reasons to hold his
fire, which was why Clint kept thinking about them when
he held off on shooting before Randy glanced too far to his
right.

After several careful steps, Randy was about to walk
back into the bushes and out of Clint's sight. Before Clint
could let out the breath he was holding, he saw Randy's
foot slip over the drop-off that led straight down into the
ditch.

Randy started to slide down the same incline that Clint
had used earlier, but he was determined to keep his eyes
focused on the spot where he'd heard that suspicious
noise. In fact, now that he'd almost stumbled, Randy
watched those bushes even more carefully as he regained
his footing.

After getting both feet beneath him, Randy scurried
ahead without making enough noise to alert a jittery deer.

"Come on," Clint whispered. "We need to get out of
here."

"But they're still close by," the woman replied. "Maybe
we should wait for a better—"

"We won't get a better chance than right now," Clint interrupted as he started climbing out the other side of the
ditch. "You either come along with me or dig in deeper
right here."

Clint wasn't even out of the ditch before he heard the
woman crawling up after him.

TWENTY-FIVE

Clint didn't have to go far to find a much better spot to hide. He and his new companion hunkered down in a nice bit of cover and merely waited for the storm to pass. Once the gunmen had moved on, they got up and stretched their legs.

"Are they gone?" she whispered.

Clint had only taken a few steps away to scout things out. When he returned, he walked up behind the woman and asked, "What was that?"

She practically jumped out of her skin and almost drew her Smith & Wesson in the process. When she finally caught her breath, she still looked like she might draw that pistol. "You scared the hell out of me," she hissed.

"Sorry about that," Clint said.

"Not that it matters, since you already forced me to make too much noise, but I guess those men are gone?"

"Yeah. They're gone."

"Good. I only hope you've got a horse somewhere nearby because they took mine."

Since they'd been hiding in a spot that put their back to a small hill and covered the rest of them in mulberry bushes, Clint needed to help her out before she cut herself to pieces. Extending a hand to her, he replied, "My horse isn't far."

"That is, if they haven't taken her like they did mine."

"It's a he," Clint corrected. "And they haven't taken him."

"How do you know that?"

"Because we would have heard the commotion if they'd tried."

It took a few moments for Clint to get his bearings again, but it wasn't long before he was retracing his steps over somewhat familiar ground. Now that they were going in a straight line instead of circling and ducking for cover, he discovered he wasn't as far away from Eclipse as he'd thought.

At first, Clint couldn't see a trace of the Darley Arabian. Then, after letting out a whistle, he heard the stallion pick his way to him. "Come on," Clint said as he took her hand and led her toward Eclipse. "The sooner we get out of these damn bushes, the better."

"Amen to that."

"There you are, boy," Clint said when he finally spotted Eclipse. After climbing into the saddle, Clint helped the woman up behind him. He then steered back toward the trail and got moving at a faster pace.

"Do me a favor and look in those saddlebags," he said after they were moving along.

The woman took a quick look and asked, "Am I looking for anything in particular?"

"Is there anything in them?"

"Not much, but a few supplies."

"Good. That's all I wanted to know."

She laughed and said, "For a man who barely escaped from being buried in the woods, you're awfully concerned about a few sticks of jerked beef and some coffee."

"It doesn't seem like a lot until you're forced to eat roots and berries for a few days."

"I suppose not. By the way, thank you for helping me out back there."

Clint shrugged. "I was in the area. I never caught your name."

"It's Carmen," she replied. "Carmen Velasquez."

Reaching over his shoulder to offer his hand, he said, "I'm Clint Adams."

She shook his hand as best she could and when she was done, she wrapped her arms a little tighter around his midsection.

"So how did you wind up in that ditch?" Clint asked.

"I was on my way to a little town you might not have even heard of. It's called Mud Foot and it's not too far from—"

"I know where it is," Clint said.

"Are you from there?"

"No."

"Then you must know this part of the country like the back of your hand to be familiar with a place like Mud Foot."

"You could say I've done more than my share of riding," Clint said.

"That's what I've been trying to do. When you grow up outside a place called Mud Foot, your first thoughts tend to drift to getting out of there. I left when I was fifteen and never looked back."

"So what happened? Did you get homesick?"

Carmen let out a tired breath. "I knew I wouldn't miss that place, but my family was still here, so I decided to pay them a visit."

"You want me to head back there so you can check in on them?"

She paused for a moment and said, "No. There's no need for that. I already checked on them." After another long pause, she added, "My parents are buried there. This is the first time I've been able to pay my respects since I heard they were dead. Now I don't care if I ever see that town again."

Even though he couldn't see her face, Clint could feel Carmen's sadness. "That explains how you got in the area," he said to steer her thoughts in another direction. "What about that ditch?"

"This place isn't the same as when I used to live here. This used to be a quiet place that seemed so far away from the rest of the world. Even though I've been through some hell since leaving home, I guess I never figured I would always be safe once I got back here.

"I used to walk in these woods all the time. My father always tried to frighten me by saying I'd get eaten by a bear, but that never worked. I wanted to walk right up to the top of these mountains."

"I know the feeling," Clint said. "This part of the country makes me want to do some wandering myself."

Carmen's arms came loose from around Clint and she held onto the lip of the saddle behind her. "I was walking along the same trail I used to walk when I was a little girl when those bastards ambushed me. I could hear them coming and I didn't do a thing about it."

"Don't fault yourself for not assuming the worst just because you heard some footsteps," Clint said as Carmen fumed behind him. "At least you weren't caught in your sleep like an idiot."

After letting out a stifled giggle, she asked, "Are you speaking from experience?"

"Sad to say, but I am. I was sleeping in my camp and I woke up with not much more than the clothes on my back. It's like they knew I'd just gotten enough supplies to last me for weeks. I didn't even hear them coming." Shifting around to get a look at her, he added, "Or going, for that matter."

Carmen's skin was the color of lightly creamed coffee. Her hair was thick and flowed over both shoulders in a way that was both wild and beautiful. Her eyes were dark as well, giving her face a dark, somewhat stern appearance. At the moment, however, her full lips were smiling and she cocked her head as if she meant to hide it from him.

Suddenly, she focused on something in front of Eclipse. "Right there," she said while pointing toward the trail ahead.

Clint turned back around and was barely able to spot a fork in the road.

"Turn off that way," she insisted.

"What's over there?"

"With any luck, my horse."

"Damn," Clint muttered. "I was just starting to enjoy this riding arrangement."

TWENTY-SIX

The fork in the road quickly narrowed down to something almost too narrow for Eclipse to use. If he was on his own, Clint would have already been looking for a spot to turn around and head back. But no matter how many times he asked Carmen if she was certain about her directions, all he got was a confident nod.

Although the branches crept in close enough to make Eclipse fret with every other step, they never stopped the Darley Arabian from moving ahead. Finally, Clint felt a pat on his shoulder.

"Stop here," Carmen said.

He pulled back on the reins and Eclipse was only too happy to oblige. Just as Clint had spotted the remains of a campfire, he felt Carmen dropping down from the saddle. She walked ahead a ways before disappearing from view.

When she came back, she was leading a black mare by the reins. From a distance, the mare might have looked similar to Eclipse from the front. The mare's body was sleeker and just a bit shorter. While she also had a splash of white to break up the solid color of her coat, the spot was on the left side of her neck instead of the nose, where Eclipse had a spot of white.

"Her name's Muriel," Carmen said while patting the mare's nose.

"Muriel? That's a name better suited for a mule."

Carmen shot Clint a mean look and said, "Muriel was my grandmother's name!"

"No offense. I just thought that horse looked more like . . ."

"Her name's fine. And if you ever want to teach that stallion of yours some humility, we can have a race."

Clint smiled. "Maybe later. Did they leave you anything in your saddlebags?"

After a quick check, Carmen replied, "Looks like I've got everything."

"Then you got off pretty light considering the men that were after you."

Carmen climbed into the saddle and took up her reins. "They found me a ways from here. Besides, they weren't exactly after my supplies when they grabbed me and threw me to the ground. If I'd been with Muriel, they never would have gotten their hands on me."

"You're lucky to have escaped."

"I'm lucky my father taught me where to kick a man when I was old enough for boys to look at me. The one who was trying to force himself on me is probably still trying to fish his balls out from where I kicked them."

Clint winced the moment he heard that. "Damn. I almost feel sorry for him."

"You should feel sorry for him if I see him again. Just because the rest of those animals didn't get their chance with me doesn't mean they deserve to try it on someone else. I don't like the thought of other children not being able to walk these trails like I did."

"Part of that might be due to the fact that folks say the mountain is cursed," Clint pointed out.

Both of them were riding back toward the main trail. Eclipse walked in front with Muriel close behind.

"Cursed?" Carmen asked. "I heard it was haunted."

"Either way, it doesn't bode well for picnics and excursions."

Carmen let out a disgusted breath. "Rumors like that were probably started because of those animals that attacked us."

"That or the train that was supposed to have been wrecked somewhere around here."

Carmen brought her horse to a stop, and Clint followed suit the moment the sound of Muriel's steps came to a halt.

"You know about that?" she asked.

"Yeah," Clint said as he shifted around to get a look at her. "Why?"

Although she tried to shrug it off, Carmen wasn't able to hide the fact that she was a little nervous. "Most people that know about that train are only here to try and find it."

"Why would anyone want to find it?"

"If you don't know, then you didn't hear the whole story."

Clint snapped his reins and got Eclipse moving again. After the stallion had taken a few steps, he could hear Carmen following along behind him. "I didn't hear the story," he said. "All I heard was that there was a train. After the time I've spent in these woods, I doubt a train could get within miles of this mountain."

"Oh, it got closer than that," Carmen replied. "But that was a while ago."

"How could any train get through all these trees?"

"First of all, it didn't roll right through this spot. It didn't even get near this part of the trail. And secondly, trees tend to grow back after they've been cut down."

Clint shook his head. "First I get robbed, then I get ambushed by those gunmen, then I get to lay in the dirt, and now I get to ride through splinter country with a smart aleck for a guide."

"A railroad got the notion of laying down some track

through here," Carmen explained after holding back a laugh at Clint's expense. "It was supposed to be a shortcut."

Now, it was time for Clint to laugh a bit. "A shortcut, huh? I'm sure that looked just fine on a map in some planner's office."

"I'll bet it did. They cleared a path and threw down some tracks. They even got the line finished, but it was too risky for it to be used by a passenger train. The story goes that only the smaller engines could get through."

Rather than share his views on the many different ways that stories could bend the truth, Clint let Carmen continue her own story.

"The trains that came through here were used to carry payrolls for the Army or gold shipments from the mountains because it was fast and there were no open spots for robbers to jump on."

"That didn't seem to stop the robbers swarming this area now," Clint pointed out.

"They're not here to rob a train," Carmen said. "They just want to find the one that crashed and took over fifty thousand dollars with it."

TWENTY-SEVEN

"So how many did we lose?"

Lou glanced around at the men gathered in the small cave they'd been using as a camp. There was no fire lit, so it took him a few minutes to pick out the dark blobs that were alive from the dark blobs that were only shadows. Once his eyes adjusted to the darkness, Lou was able to get something of an accurate count.

"Well, Joey's gone," Lou said.

Jack's eyes narrowed as he pulled down the bandanna that had been covering the bottom portion of his face. Everything below his nose was in fairly good shape, but everything above that was covered with scratches in all shapes and sizes. Like the rest of the men, he'd paid the price for running so quickly through the thick woods.

"I know Joey's gone," Jack snarled. "I was there! I saw the big son of a bitch get shot to pieces and drop right in front of me!"

"I was just saying—"

"Well, say something I don't already know!"

"Randy and Hank checked in and went back out already," Lou said. "One of them was hurt. I think it was Hank."

"What's wrong with him?"

"He caught a bullet when . . . well . . . you know."

Although Joey wasn't the center of the group, he was the one that all of the others counted on in a fight. Actually, he was the one that all the others wanted to have in front of them in a fight. Losing him was like losing the biggest weapon in their arsenal and was still a touchy subject for the group's leader.

Jack nodded and motioned for Lou to continue.

"There were a few others who got wounded," Lou said. "I haven't heard from or seen Chris or Will since we started this whole chase earlier today."

"Speaking of that chase, do you have anything to say about that?"

"Only that we're still chasing."

"Still chasing," Jack said in a dry tone of voice that didn't sound the least bit impressed. "That's just great. And whose idea was it to start that chase to begin with? Didn't I tell everyone to keep their heads out of their asses so we could get what we came here for?"

"All due respect, but that could just be a legend."

Jack lunged forward and took hold of Lou using his bad arm. He practically pulled the man out of his boots, and didn't stop until Lou was struggling to keep his balance.

"If you want to call me stupid," Jack snarled, "then go on and say it."

Lou was quick to shake his head, even though it meant losing a little more of his balance. "No, no. That's not what I meant at all."

"Then what did you mean to say? You want to say that I've kept us away from the law, God only knows how many posses, and twice as many vigilante hunting parties just to lead us into a wall now?"

With Jack's voice booming through the cave, it was hard for Lou to think straight. When he looked around to some of the other men who were in there, all he got were a few blank stares and some quickly averted glances.

"I'm just saying that we've been doing real good up to now," Lou explained. "And even though we got a trail to follow, that don't mean it'll lead us to some broken-down buried treasure."

"The train went through here," Jack snarled. "We know that for a fact. All we got to do is find it and everything we've gone through will be worth it."

Lou lowered his voice and said, "But we could make more money taking down a few banks."

"When we lost Joey," Jack replied in an equally low voice, "all of our shares went up. That's making money in my book. Besides, we know there's at least fifty grand in that mountain. There could always be more. My gut tells me there's a lot more. Otherwise, I wouldn't have had to kill so many federals to get my hands on this telegram."

When he said that last part, Jack patted the shirt pocket where he kept the telegram in question. Lou sat silently for a few moments so he could measure his words before saying them.

"Did that actually say how much money was on that train when it crashed?" Lou asked.

Jack's eyes narrowed into slits and he fixed them on Lou. "You still don't trust me?"

"That ain't it at all."

Jack leaned forward in a quick, smooth motion that was something like a snake moving through the weeds without disturbing a single one. "I say there's money to be had and that means there's money to be had," he whispered just loud enough for Lou to hear. "If you want to second-guess me in front of my men, you're setting yourself up for one hell of a fall."

Shaking his head, Lou started to back away. Just as his shoulder bumped against the cave's wall, he felt Jack's hand snap out to clamp around his shoulder.

Jack pulled the other man in and added, "You don't need to say this kind of shit after we saw one of our own get killed. There's wounded men nearby and I ain't about to let you fill their heads with this kind of doubting bullshit."

"I . . . I didn't . . ."

"Just keep your fucking mouth shut unless I ask you to open it from here on in. You understand?"

Since he was unable to spit out any more words, Lou nodded again.

When Jack let go of him, he made sure to bounce Lou off the wall hard enough for the sound to echo all the way back into the cave. He then turned to look at each of the men that were huddled nearby.

"Whoever that asshole is that shot Joey will pay for what he done," Jack announced. "Whether he's after the same money we are or not, him and that other one will be buried on this goddamn mountain. We'll gut both of them and leave them for the maggots!"

The men didn't let out a cheer or even make much noise at all, but they did get determined, murderous looks in their eyes as they nodded to what they'd heard.

Jack smiled beneath the curtain of greasy hair that had all but covered his face. He liked what he saw.

TWENTY-EIGHT

"So there's supposed to be fifty thousand on this train that crashed?" Clint asked as he rode alongside Carmen.

She nodded and shifted in the saddle to accommodate the movements of her horse. After making it back to the main trail, they'd been able to ride side by side instead of single file. There wasn't much room to spare, but at least they could see each other when they talked.

"Fifty thousand," Carmen repeated. "Some say a hundred thousand. I even heard there was supposed to be a couple hundred thousand in gold, but I don't know how much of that I believe."

"It could make sense. I mean, anyone transporting that much money would want to do it in secret rather than take their chances on getting robbed along the regular railroad lines. Then again, it would seem that someone transporting something so valuable would be a little safer with their investment." Clint shook his head and smirked. "I guess this is how rumors are started, huh?"

Carmen nodded and kept her eyes pointed straight ahead. After a few moments, she turned to Clint and asked, "So is that why you're here?"

"To start rumors?"

"No. To look in on one."

Clint shrugged. "Tell you the truth, this whole thing about the train is news to me."

"Is it?"

"Yeah," he replied while looking over at her to study her face a bit more carefully. "It is."

"So why are you out here then? And don't tell me you were just passing through. I used to live here and I know that nobody just passes through woods like these."

"Actually, I'm looking for some friends of mine."

"Would I know them?" she asked.

"I couldn't say. Do you know anyone named Jebediah Cobbler or Melvin Grimley?"

Smirking, Carmen replied, "I'm sure I wouldn't be able to forget names like those."

"Well, I know Jebediah lived in Mud Foot. I'm surprised you haven't heard of him."

"I've been away for a while. Remember?"

"That's right," Clint said as he shifted to watch the road in front of him. "You mentioned that."

"Those two must be good friends for you to come all the way out here and go through so much trouble to find them."

"Well, you never know what might happen when you're out riding in this mess. Nobody's heard from them in a while and I found out they might be headed in this direction."

"Maybe I can help," Carmen offered.

"You're not in a hurry to get out of here?"

"I don't really have anywhere else to go." She kept her eyes pointing forward, but looked over after a few moments of dead silence from Clint. When she looked over at him, she found that he was staring at her intently. "All right," she said finally. "Maybe I do recognize one of those names."

"I suspected as much."

"What gave me away?"

Rather than admit he was working off nothing but a

blind hunch, Clint tilted his head and looked away as if he was holding onto a secret that was too good to let go just yet. That tricked worked pretty well in poker, and it seemed to be doing just as well now.

After squirming for a bit, Carmen said, "There's always been a Cobbler living in Mud Foot. The name Jebediah rings a few bells, but I don't know if I've ever met him."

"Then how do you think you could help find him?"

Carmen pulled back on her reins and brought her horse to a stop. Clint followed suit and brought Eclipse back a few steps so he could look straight into her eyes.

"If you've got something to say, just say it," she demanded. "I'm grateful that you helped me out of that ditch, but if you don't want my company any longer, just say the word and I'll go."

"I'll be more than happy to ride with you, but there's something you're not telling me. And don't bother denying it because I've looked into enough lying eyes to recognize a pair when I see them."

There was plenty of anger in her eyes, but that soon faded. Carmen quickly looked away and gave her reins a gentle flick. The mare started walking, but it was more of a slow mosey than anything else.

"I've told you everything," she said.

Before the mare could get too far away, Clint reached out to take hold of her reins. When she felt the resistance, Muriel came to a stop and shook her head. Carmen looked surprised at Clint's move, but not overly so.

"All right," Clint said. "Let me tell you what's on my mind and then maybe you can let me know what's on yours. First of all, I may not know these woods like the back of my hand, but I've got eyes in my head." Pointing a finger straight ahead and up, he added, "And I can see that we're riding straight for Farewell Mountain."

When Carmen glanced to where Clint was pointing, the expression on her face remained cool and distant.

"And second?" she asked. "When you start off saying first, there's got to be a second."

Clint pulled back his arm, held up the finger he'd been pointing, and lifted another finger to join it. "Second, you're riding awfully slow for someone who narrowly escaped getting killed or worse no more than an hour ago."

Carmen's head hung low and she turned so she didn't even have to see a part of him. When she was able to face Clint again, she steeled herself and straightened up in her saddle. "You're right on both counts."

"I know I am. I was hoping for a bit of explanation."

"I have heard Jeremiah Cobbler's name before," she admitted. "I overheard some of those men were talking about him right before I was attacked."

"What did they say?"

After pulling in a breath, she replied, "That they were going to hunt him down and kill him."

TWENTY-NINE

Clint let out a measured breath and looked away from her. When he looked back, he did his level best to keep his own face as passive as Carmen's was at the moment. "Is this about that train?" he asked.

"I don't know. All I know is that I heard them talking about it just before they spotted me. After that, I was too busy running and hiding to pick up on much else. If he's your friend, I'm sorry, but he might already be dead."

While that settled in his brain like silt drifting to the bottom of a lake, Clint looked at the mountain that loomed ahead of them. He'd certainly seen more impressive mountains, but this one had seemed to rush up on him like it had legs of its own. The last time he'd caught sight of it, he'd sworn it was at least a day's ride away. Now, he felt like he could reach out and write his initials in the snowcaps.

"And I suppose you were planning on heading to that mountain to check up on those rumors for yourself?" he asked.

"The thought crossed my mind. Like you said, I know these woods like the back of my hand. I figured if nothing panned out, I could just head back." Taking some of the edge from her voice, she added, "If you'd want to come along with me, I could cut you in on whatever profits there are."

"And what happens if all of this turns out to be some sort of campfire story?"

"Then we part ways."

Clint laughed under his breath and said, "That's certainly not the most appealing offer I've ever gotten."

"You've already come this far," she said quickly. "Your friend is out here and he was headed for that mountain. If you're looking for him, that's where you'd be going anyway. You might find him or you might just find a share of fifty thousand dollars."

"Or I might come up empty."

"True."

"Or," Clint added before Carmen could go on with her pitch, "I could cross paths with those killers that are crawling through these woods like worms through turned soil."

"I suppose there's that too. But I'd be taking that same risk, you know. Besides, we've both already met up with those killers and we're still alive to talk about it. How much worse could it get?"

Clint looked over at her with half a smile on his face. "That's just the sort of question you never want to ask."

It wasn't far to the base of the mountain, but the trail wound so much that it took them a good portion of the day to get there. By the time Clint felt the ground start to slope upward, it was early in the evening. Both he and Carmen looked like the men they'd managed to avoid all day since both of their faces were covered by bandannas. Even that didn't keep them from collecting a good amount of scrapes and scratches on their heads and necks.

"We should start looking for a spot to camp," Clint said. "Do you know any good places around here?"

Carmen stood up in her stirrups and took a look around. "It's been a while since I've camped this far out, so your guess is as good as mine."

"Well, I haven't had much luck in picking safe camping spots," he said while steering Eclipse to the side of the trail. "So be my guest."

Flicking the reins, Carmen moved ahead and soon rode off the trail. She quickly reappeared and motioned for Clint to follow her.

Eclipse grumbled and let out some dissatisfied snuffs as his sides were scratched and poked by the ever-present branches. Before too long, the Darley Arabian stepped through and into something close to a clearing. Although it wasn't exactly an open spot, it was hidden from the main trail and big enough for both riders and their horses.

"How's this?" Carmen asked.

Clint was already climbing down from his saddle and stretching his legs. "Good enough for me. Once we clear it out a bit, we'll have more than enough kindling for a fire."

"You want to make a fire? With those men still out there?"

"Just a little one to cook some food and boil some water. Besides, these damn branches are thick enough for us to dance around waving torches over our heads without being seen."

"Good point. Let's get to work."

The clearing was small enough for the two of them to gather up most of the stray branches in a few minutes. What was left was either connected to a nearby tree or stuck in the dirt like a gnarled root. Clint fished some supplies out of his saddlebag while Carmen got the fire going.

"So how long have you known Jebediah?" she asked.

"Actually, I met him not too long ago over a game of cards."

Shaking her head while working a few handfuls of leaves into the fire, she replied, "All this trouble for someone you just played cards with? That must have been a hell of a game."

"It was," Clint said as he stood between Eclipse and Muriel while trying not to get stepped on.

"Did you win, at least?"

"Nope. But I lost a lot less than someone else did."

"That's right. Melvin was his name, wasn't it? Was he at the game too?"

"Sure was."

"Maybe I should start playing cards more. Seems like a good way to meet people."

Making sure that he wasn't being watched, Clint closed the flap of Carmen's saddlebag and then did the same for his own. "Nah. They're just the type of people who get you into trouble."

She laughed and turned to look over her shoulder. "I guess," she said with an inviting smile. "But I seem to have done pretty well just by falling into a ditch."

"We'll just wait and see if you still think that after we part ways."

THIRTY

Clint sat with his back against a tree and his eyes fixed upon the sputtering remains of the fire. Once the sun got close to the horizon, the thick layers of trees seemed to wipe away the light. Soon, they were surrounded by a darkness that felt like a tangible thing. Shadows crept in like spilled soup and the air grew stickier with each passing minute.

When he heard approaching footsteps, Clint barely moved. His eyes flicked in that direction, but flicked back the moment he saw the familiar figure walk in from the trees.

"I scouted ahead a ways," Carmen said as she took a seat next to Clint.

"Let me guess," Clint said. "You found a bunch of trees?"

"Pretty much." She studied him for a moment and frowned. "What's the matter with you?"

"I'm thinking. Actually," he said while prodding one of the embers inside the fire, "I was trying to remember something."

"What was it?"

He closed his eyes and imagined the same image that

had been in his mind since Carmen had left to take a look around. Although he could recall most everything that had happened during that card game, one detail kept slipping away from him.

"I got a look at that deed," he told her.

"The one that Jebediah won?"

"Yeah. I got a look at it and I remember that it was genuine, but that's about it. If I could remember something else that was on there, I might be able to narrow down our search a bit. Otherwise, we've got the whole damn mountain to choose from."

"Well, it's not the biggest mountain around," she offered. "At least that's in our favor."

Clint smiled and pressed his fingertips to his eyes to relieve some of the pressure. It was a humid night and that made his skin feel uncomfortable. "The more I try to think about this, the further away it gets."

"Then stop thinking about it," Carmen said while reaching out to take hold of Clint's wrist. Once she pulled his hand away, she managed to lower his arm. From there, she reached up with her other hand to turn Clint's face toward her. "Maybe I can give you something better to think about."

Clint looked at her for no more than a moment or two. That was all the time he needed to see the hunger in her eyes and feel the warmth in her touch. It was the kind of warmth that had nothing to do with the humidity in the air or the heat of a summer night.

"This isn't clearing my head too well," Clint whispered as he leaned forward. "In fact, it's giving me a whole bunch of other ideas."

Carmen smiled and tilted her head just enough for her bottom lip to brush against Clint's chin. "Really?" she asked while easing her mouth up over Clint's. "And what kind of ideas might those be?"

"Ideas like this," he said while reaching out to wrap an

arm around Carmen so he could pull her closer. With another pull and some help from her, Clint wound up with Carmen sitting across his lap. "Or this," he said.

Her body was slender. The muscles under her skin were tight and tense. Her hair smelled like the night itself, and her darkened skin made the dim light from the fire mix perfectly with the soft pale glow of the moon. When Clint reached out to tug at the leather laces holding her buckskins together, she squirmed a bit to make it easier for him.

"Seems like you've been working on this idea of yours for a little while," she said.

"You'd be surprised how many ideas are running through my head right now. And it all started when I first felt those lips of yours."

"You mean these?" she asked innocently as she brushed her mouth against Clint's ear.

When she whispered to him, Carmen's breath was another touch of heat against Clint's skin. "Because if you think that's soft, you haven't felt anything yet."

Before he knew what he was doing, Clint had Carmen wrapped up in his arms and was kissing her deeply on the mouth. Her body conformed perfectly to his and she settled onto his lap. After a bit of rearranging her limbs, Carmen was sitting with her arms and legs around him and looking him straight in the eyes.

Clint cupped her tight buttocks in his hands, savoring the way they felt in the buckskins. Even though he'd pulled out the leather cords, they were still tight enough to cling to her body. That turned out to be a good thing because peeling those clothes off her turned out to be a pleasure in itself.

As Clint stripped the buckskins off her, he could feel that she wasn't just talking before. Her skin was smooth as silk under those clothes and his hands began wandering over her as if they had a mind of their own. He traced a line down the curve of her spine until he finally worked his way to the supple curve of her backside.

As she felt him touch her, Carmen shifted and squirmed in Clint's lap. Her hands remained locked around his neck as she rubbed her legs along his side. After one final tug, the leather cord cinching up the front of her pants came loose and she was able to kick them off with ease.

Carmen smiled widely as she leaned back so Clint could pull her pants the rest of the way off. "When I put these on," she said, "I didn't know it would be such a trick to get them off."

The firelight danced over Carmen's naked skin, making every one of her curves stand out in the twitching shadows. Her hair was splayed carelessly behind her and she licked her lips in anticipation while watching Clint approach her.

Clint was on his knees and shucking off his own clothes. "Don't worry," he said. "It looks like it'll be plenty worth the effort."

THIRTY-ONE

The fire was nothing more than a few glowing embers and one stubborn spark. As that spark faded out, it left Clint and Carmen in the shadows. Carmen was standing with her hands pressed against a tree trunk and her back to Clint. As Clint moved behind her, she arched her back into a slope that ended with the smooth curve of her backside.

Clint couldn't see more than the outline of her body, but that only forced him to seek her out with every one of his other senses. He could smell a faint hint of her skin and could hear her breathing with quick anticipation.

His hands roamed up and down her back and hips until he couldn't hold off any longer. As he took half a step forward, he could feel Carmen spreading her legs further apart so his rigid penis could slide between them. After a few back-and-forth strokes, the tip of his cock found the wet, soft lips of her pussy and slipped between them with ease.

Carmen's grip tightened on the tree until her nails dug into the bark. She turned to look over her shoulder at Clint, and could just make out his head and shoulders as he started pumping in and out of her. His erection grew harder with each thrust, filling her more and more every time until she was moaning all the way from the back of her throat.

As Clint's eyes adjusted to the dark, he could see more details of her finely toned body. She had the build of a true rider. Her hips were trim and narrow and her thighs were strong. When she perched herself up on her tiptoes, the muscles all along the back of her legs tensed beautifully.

Their eyes met and locked onto one another. In that moment, they could see each other perfectly. In that moment, nothing else around them mattered more than the feel of Clint inside her and the little gasps of pleasure Carmen would occasionally let slip.

Taking hold of her hips in both hands, Clint started pumping into her even harder. Whenever he pounded into her, he could see Carmen biting down on her lower lip to keep from making any more noise. His bare feet dug into the moist soil as Carmen's fingers dug into the thick bark.

Soon, she was sliding her hands up along the tree while stretching her back. That new angle allowed Clint to slide into her in a slightly different way. When he was buried all the way in, she felt her heart skip a beat.

Carmen wriggled against Clint as he pumped into her from behind. When she felt his arms wrap around her midsection, she reached behind to brush her fingers against Clint's sides. Before too long, that wasn't enough to keep her happy and she started turning around to face him. Although Clint longed to be inside her the minute he came out, he was glad to see her from the front with the moonlight washing over her skin.

"I need to get my hands on you," she said.

With those words still hanging in the air, they embraced and let their hands roam freely over each other's body. They lowered themselves to the ground so Clint could quickly spread out his bedroll. Carmen lay on top of it and spread her legs open wide, anxiously waiting to feel him again.

Although Clint dropped down to his knees and quickly moved to position himself, she wasn't able to wait for him. Carmen leaned back and moved one hand over her hard nipples while the other hand slipped between her legs.

The moment her fingers found her clit, she started moaning again. Moving her hand in little circles, she started writhing against the blanket. Clint found himself watching her and enjoying the sight of Carmen pleasuring herself. His hands wandered up and down her legs, but he kept from doing any more.

The last thing he wanted to do just then was make her stop.

Suddenly, Carmen's eyes snapped open and she sat up just enough to grab Clint's hand. "I want you," she moaned. "Don't make me wait." As she lay back down again, she pulled Clint on top of her. Although she'd spread her legs open wider, she clamped them tightly around him the moment she felt his cock brush against the lips of her pussy.

Before Clint could make another move, he felt her hand guiding him into her. The moment he was inside, Carmen pumped her hips off the blanket to get him all the way in. She thrust her hips back and forth while watching the expression on his face as she quickened her pace.

Clint stayed where he was and enjoyed what she was doing. His hands closed tightly around the blanket as her wet pussy glided faster and faster along the length of his cock. When she pumped her hips forward and kept them there, Carmen let out a long, satisfied breath.

She was just on the verge of a climax. Clint could tell that much by the way she pulled in quick, shallow breaths, and even by the way she looked at him. The hunger in her eyes had become tempered with a more urgent need that struck much deeper than wanting him.

She needed him.

Straightening up so he was upright and still on his knees, Clint reached down to grab her tight backside and hold her in place. Now it was his turn to take control and that was exactly what he did. As he massaged Carmen's firm, rounded ass, he began thrusting into her in a new rhythm.

It was slow at first, but quickly became a faster pounding. Then, just as she was starting to breathe even quicker, he slowed down to a crawl. As he lingered with just the tip of his penis in her, Clint could see a tortured expression growing on her face. Then, just as she was about to beg him to go on, he started pumping almost as quickly as he could.

Their bodies came together urgently and furiously.

Carmen arched her back as one orgasm led straight into another. Each one was more powerful than the last, until her eyes were clenched shut and she was clawing at the ground on either side of the blanket.

As he thrust his hips forward, Clint pulled her to him. He could feel Carmen's muscles growing weak until his hands were the only things holding her up. Slowing to a more leisurely pace, Clint savored the way her smooth, moist lips wrapped around him. Her body was hot and wet and took every inch of him inside.

Once he let his eyes linger on the way the sweat trickled along her naked breasts and the enticing lines of her stomach as she leaned back in front of him, he could feel his own climax approaching. Carmen let out a few breathless words as he pumped into her harder again.

THIRTY-TWO

It was a few hours later before Carmen so much as moved from the spot where she'd collapsed. She got up without making a sound, quickly gathering up her clothes and putting them on. All the while, she kept her eyes on Clint. Once she was satisfied that he wasn't going to wake up anytime soon, she slipped away from the camp.

Clint waited until he could no longer hear her footsteps before making a move. Although he might have drifted off to sleep quite easily after all that activity, these were not normal circumstances. Not only was he still feeling the sting of being robbed so easily several days ago, but he'd never forgotten about the gunmen that were patrolling the area.

Whether or not he believed there was a train and its supposed treasure didn't matter. There were plenty of men out there who did believe, and they were all carrying guns. Considering all of that, Clint was surprised he'd been able to relax enough to even look like he was sleeping.

As it was, he managed to stretch out, keep his eyes closed, and stay still without drifting off. He'd even gotten some rest while keeping at least one eye partially open at all times. And just when he'd been starting to think he was too untrusting for his own good, his suspicions had paid off.

Then again, seeing Carmen sneak away like that wasn't exactly the payoff he would have preferred. Still, it wasn't exactly unexpected.

He was dressed and buckling on his gun belt in less than a minute. Clint no longer needed a fire to see where he was going within the small clearing. After taking a few steps into the surrounding trees, he could see only one of the larger shapes in the darkness where there had previously been two.

Clint reached out to pat the single horse's nose, which was more than enough to tell him it was Eclipse. And since Carmen had bothered to risk taking her horse when she was sneaking off, that meant she had a ways to go and precious little time to get there.

Before Clint could decide what to do in the time that left him, he heard something that made his heart jump into the back of his throat. Someone else was sneaking around in the bushes, creeping steadily toward Clint.

Without moving his feet from where they were, Clint twisted the rest of his body around to face the sound of the oncoming steps. The only sound he made was the whisper of iron against leather as he drew the modified Colt and waited for a target to present itself.

After a few seconds, Clint spotted something moving that wasn't a bunch of branches swaying in the breeze. It was something much more solid and too tall to be an animal of the four-legged variety. Narrowing his eyes to try and get an even better look before that animal got too much closer, Clint found himself crouching down and holding his breath.

The man was slightly taller than average and had a good amount of meat on his bones. His clothes were a tattered mess and his eyes were wide enough to catch what little moonlight had made it through the canopy of trees. Although he carried a gun in his hands, he was swinging it back and forth between so many different targets that there was no way for him to hit one.

The closer he got to Clint's spot, the more his arms and legs got tangled up in the bushes. That was one of the reasons Clint liked the spot they'd chosen for camp, and he took advantage of all that noise by moving quickly in the midst of it.

The man's breathing was heavy as he reached out to pull aside a particularly bothersome mess of branches. When he heard the first sign of movement, he choked down his next breath and raised his gun to just above hip level. At least, he would have been able to raise it that high if it didn't get snagged on the same branches that had caught his legs.

"Shit," the man whispered as he pulled the gun free. When he finally got it loose, he stumbled forward and shoved the gun out to point right between the eyes that he'd spotted in the darkness.

When Eclipse saw the man practically fall toward him, the Darley Arabian backed up and used his front legs to swipe at him.

The man stumbled back again to avoid the horse's hooves, and immediately backed into something much more solid than bushes.

"Drop the gun and raise your hands," Clint whispered as he pressed the Colt's barrel into the small of the man's back.

The man did as he was told and turned around. When he saw Clint's face, Jeb immediately let out a relieved breath. "Jesus, Clint, am I glad to see you."

THIRTY-THREE

After being wound up so tightly, it took a few seconds for Clint to lower his gun. In those seconds, the relief on Jeb's face shifted to pure terror. Finally, the relief came back when the Colt found its way back into Clint's holster.

"What the hell are you doing sneaking around out here?" Clint asked in something close to a snarl.

"I've been out here for . . . I don't even know how long."

Before Jeb could say another word, Clint was motioning for him to lower his voice as well as his gun. Jeb glanced around nervously before he remembered that he even had a gun in his hand. As he lowered the weapon, he found himself being dragged away from the camp.

Clint shoved Jeb between two thick trees and told him to stay put. After that, he circled the area twice just to make certain that there wasn't anyone else lurking in the shadows. When he came back to where Jeb was waiting, Clint made sure that he was facing the camp so he could see if Carmen was on her way back.

"What the hell happened to you?" Clint asked. "As far as anyone else is concerned, you just disappeared."

"I didn't mean to disappear. I just had to leave."

"Why? What happened?"

129

Jeb took a few deep breaths and allowed himself to drop down into a sitting position. His legs were bent in front of him and his arms dropped onto his lap, making him look like a doll that had been tossed into a corner. His eyes weren't as wide as they had been when Clint had found him, but they were awfully close.

Slowing his voice and taking some of the edge from it, Clint said, "I heard that you were attacked outside of the bank."

"Yeah," Jeb said as he brought his eyes up to fix upon Clint. "I was."

"What happened?"

"It was Melvin. He walked up to me as I was headed for the bank to pay off the loan for my house. He said that I cheated and that I needed to pay him back what he lost. I told him that I couldn't and kept walking."

Jeb pulled in a few more breaths since they were starting to come a little easier. "I got to the bank, but Melvin kept pestering me. He was calling me a cheater, and even said that you and me were together in taking all his money along with that deed."

"What deed was that?" Clint asked, even though he could still recall most of the writing for himself.

"It's a deed for a patch of land on the side of Farewell Mountain. I thought it might be for a mine or something, but it's not."

"It isn't? Are you sure about that?"

Jeb nodded. "Melvin and I had some more words outside the bank. He even went so far as to try and pull a gun on me to make me give back what I won. I swear I don't know what got into me, but all I could think about was losing my home and maybe even my life.

"I didn't know I had it in me, but I came at him and intended on taking that gun away from him." Lowering his head, he added, "I even thought of using that gun on him for all the trouble him and the rest have caused me."

"Did Abe or his brother have anything to do with this?" Clint asked.

Shaking his head, Jeb replied, "Not that I know of. But Abe's done plenty and just when I thought it was over, along comes that other big mouth to call me a cheater and Lord knows what else. Me and Melvin tussled in that alley and I damn near got that gun away from him.

"Before I knew what happened, he kicked me where it hurt the most and pointed that gun right in my face. He took every cent I had, Mr. Adams. Every damn penny. But he acted like that wasn't enough. He kept saying he wanted that deed because it was his and he didn't deserve to lose it."

"But you didn't give it to him?"

"No. I didn't have it on me at the time, but I told him that I sold it." He shifted in his spot uncomfortably before adding, "I told him I sold it to you."

That didn't affect Clint half as much as Jeb thought it would. Judging by the look on Jeb's face, he was expecting Clint to explode at any second.

"Sorry about that," Jeb said with a shrug. "I didn't want him to think I still had that deed and I thought you were already out of town."

"Nothing for you to be sorry about. I *was* out of town."

"Then what are you doing back here?" After thinking it over for a second, Jeb cringed and quickly added, "Not that I mean to pry."

"Don't worry," Clint assured him. "If I was in with the rest of these gunmen, you would have known about it by now."

Jeb let out a breath.

"Do you buy in to what folks say about Farewell Mountain?" Clint asked.

"I know that plenty of men have gone up there and were never seen again. I also know the country is rough enough in these parts to swallow up men like a hungry bear."

"That's not what I meant."

"Oh, you heard the story about the trains?"

Clint nodded. "Only I heard there was just one train in particular that everyone was concerned about."

"The story changes depending on who you ask. I heard so many different ones that they don't hardly mean much anymore. Tell you the truth, I stopped listening a long while ago."

"Then why go through so much trouble to keep that deed?"

The way he shook his head and rolled his eyes, Jeb had been asking himself that very question more times than he could count. "When Melvin first walked up to me and said the things he did, I just wanted to keep it so he didn't have it. That loudmouthed asshole got on my nerves during that game and I was glad to beat him when it was all said and done."

Clint laughed. "Trust me, you weren't the only one who was glad to see him fall."

"That wasn't even the first game I had with him. He's beaten me a few times and I've beaten him, but he never once talked to me like I was a man and not some idiot. That last game, he wanted to break me in half. I could feel it. Hell, I almost thought he'd done it until that last card was dealt.

"But when it was said and done, I won," Jeb recalled, as if he could still hardly believe it. "I won and it was great. Then there was that trouble with Abe, and by the time Melvin pushed me into that alley, I thought for sure I was cursed for something I done in my life."

Jeb's eyes were pointed in Clint's direction, but it was plain to see that he wasn't looking at anything in particular. Instead, he seemed to be lost in his own memories as he spoke in a tired monotone. "I kept that deed just so I wouldn't lose everything. It was hid in my house and not long after I went to get it, that house wasn't mine no more.

"That was the worst thing I could imagine happening and when it did, I didn't know what else to do. All I had left was a deed to some patch of land on a mountain that was supposed to be cursed. Since that was all I had to my name, I thought I'd come out here and see what I could do with that land."

"You came out here to live on Farewell Mountain?" Clint asked.

Jeb shrugged and nodded. "I got nowhere else to go and no money to spend, so that seemed like the only thing left for me to do. I've used my own two hands to make my living for as long as I can remember. There's plenty around here for building and plenty of animals to shoot. A man could do worse."

"Do you know who these gunmen are or why they're prowling through these woods?" Clint asked.

"Yeah," Jeb replied. "They're the ones giving Farewell Mountain its bad reputation."

THIRTY-FOUR

Once Jeb got his heart beating at its normal pace and recovered from the initial shock of his run-in with Clint, he had plenty more to say. Most of that was about his journey into the woods and his trip up the mountain. For the moment, however, Clint was much more interested in hearing what he had to say about the gunmen.

Jeb was more than happy to talk about them. "I can do better than that," he offered. "I can take you right to them."

"That's not a good idea," Clint said. "But you could point me in the right direction."

"I've gotten real good at keeping quiet and sneaking around, Mr. Adams. These woods are real easy to get lost in. I nearly got lost myself and I've lived a few miles away for a good portion of my life."

"No offense, Jeb, but you didn't have much luck in sneaking past me. If I was one of those gunmen, you'd be dead and buried right about now."

"No offense taken. But if you were one of those gunmen, you never would have seen me. I've snuck by them plenty of times. Besides," he added with a proud grin, "I found you just fine, didn't I?"

Clint chuckled. "You got lucky on that account."

"The hell I did. Actually I . . ." He drifted off for a moment and shifted on his feet. "I could . . . um . . . hear you two a little ways off."

"How far off?"

"About fifteen yards. Maybe twenty."

Shrugging, Clint said, "That's not too bad considering how thick these trees are."

For a moment or two, Jeb merely stared at Clint as if he didn't quite know what to think. Then, he cut loose with a laugh, which he quickly had to suppress before it got too loud. Clint laughed a bit too, enjoying the calm before the approaching storm.

"Honestly, though, Mr. Adams. I can do more for you than just point you in the right direction. I'll do whatever you say, just so long as I can do something to get these men out of here."

"Are you after revenge for what Melvin did to you?"

"I'm not the vengeful sort. It's just that, this mountain is the only place left I can call home. There's nothing left for me in town and I'll be damned if I'll let myself get run out of two places in one week."

Despite the certainty in Jeb's voice, Clint couldn't stop thinking about the loud steps he'd heard and the shakiness in Jeb's gun arm. Also, there was something else that gave him reason to play things a little closer to the vest.

"All right," Clint finally said. "You can take me to them, but you've got to listen to everything I say and do everything I tell you to do."

"Oh, I will," Jeb said with a quick nod.

"If I tell you to turn tail and run, you do just that. It's either that or wind up dead." Clint could see the chill run through Jeb's face when he heard that last part. "Now, if you want to just point me in the right direction and be done with it, there's no shame."

"I've already been pushed around enough, Mr. Adams. Whether Melvin is with them others or not, I won't be pushed any further. Besides, I ain't got much to lose."

Although Clint had some reservations, he kept them to himself. Desperate men could be capable of great things, but they could also be one hell of a liability in a fight. In the end, Clint decided it was better to keep this desperate man in sight rather than have him running around on his own.

"How far away are they?" Clint asked.

"Less than a quarter mile up this road."

Looking to where Jeb was pointing, Clint didn't even see a road. "Lead on," he said, hoping he hadn't made a mistake in not sending Jeb away.

It turned out that Jeb knew what he was talking about. At least, the road he'd mentioned truly did exist. Like the other roads that Clint had found in those woods, it wasn't much more than a half-cleared path through the tangle of leaves. It also meandered more than a drunken snake, but Jeb seemed to have complete faith in where it was headed.

No matter how many twists and turns the road took, it allowed them to move a lot faster than if they were picking their way through the bushes. They covered a good amount of ground in a short amount of time. Soon, Jeb was motioning for them to stop.

"Right down that way," Jeb whispered while pointing into the shadows.

THIRTY-FIVE

Clint leaned forward and strained his senses to see if he could pick up on what Jeb was pointing at. Just as he was about to give up, he caught a faint flicker of light followed by the wispy curl of smoke drifting through the air.

"Remember, Jeb," Clint whispered. "Stay low and do what I say. From here on in, if you've got something to tell me, point or give a signal. We need to keep quiet."

"Yes, sir, Mr.—" Jeb caught himself before saying another word. With a quick nod, he turned the key to an invisible lock right in front of his mouth.

Since it was too late to second-guess himself, Clint hoped Jeb knew how to use the gun he'd brought, and moved ahead.

It seemed the gunmen had had the same idea as Clint where the campfire was concerned. The one in the middle of their camp gave off less light than some lanterns, and crackled with the effort to stay alive. Clint was ready to be outgunned from the moment he set out to find that camp. He was even ready to be forced to fight his way out and do his best to keep Jeb alive in the process. When he saw there were only two men sitting around that fire, his hopes picked up.

During the last chase through those woods, Clint had heard plenty of names get tossed back and forth. He'd also seen glimpses of plenty of faces. This time, only one of the faces around the fire was familiar, and he couldn't match it to a name.

Clint signaled for Jeb to stay put and then got a nod as a reply. After that, he hunkered down as low as he could get and then eased his way closer to the fire. Between the rustle of the wind through the leaves and the voices of the men themselves, Clint was able to creep along at a fairly good pace.

"Was that Hank who came by while I was taking a piss?" the first gunman asked.

"Nah. It was Chris."

Those two gunmen looked similar to the rest in that they were covered in dirt, had plenty of scratches on their faces, and had a chin full of scraggly whiskers. The first one was slightly bigger than the second and had a solid, protruding belly. The second made up for the size difference by carrying an extra pistol around his waist.

"I thought Chris was shot," the first one said as he poked one of the dew glowing embers.

"Nope."

"With the way Jack's been going on, it seems like we all might get shot before this is over."

"Jack won't shoot none of us," the second gunman said.

The first one shrugged and spit onto the ground beside him. "I seen him get worked up one time where he pulled a gun and nearly blew Lou's head off."

"I wish he would blow Lou's head off. That asshole gets on my nerves."

"Yeah, well, it'll be worth putting up with him if we get half as rich as Jack is promising. You really think he's set to find that money?"

"That's what him and Chris are supposed to talk about."

"I didn't even think that was more than a bunch of old wives' tales," the first man grunted.

The second one got up and dusted himself off. "Guess we'll all find out soon enough. I'll be right back."

"There's a real good tree that'a way. I marked it for ya."

"How about I mark you?" With that, the gunman started tugging on his trousers while walking away from the fire. He relieved himself on the first spot he could find that struck his fancy, rearranged his trousers, and then walked back.

He hadn't been gone for more than a minute, but his partner had disappeared.

"Will? Where the hell are you?"

Squinting to try and make use of what little light the campfire offered, the second gunman stepped into the little clearing and turned around like a dog getting ready to have a seat. When he came full circle, he spotted a couple of odd shapes at the edge of camp.

There were two of them right next to each other. Both shapes were dark, roughly oval in shape, and hadn't been there when he'd left. In fact, the more he studied them, the more the shapes looked like boots.

"This ain't no time for games, Will," the gunman said, doing his best to sound at ease. He wasn't doing a very good job.

After taking a few more steps, he was already close enough to reach out and touch those two things at the edge of camp. Not only did they look like boots, but they felt like boots when he gave them a tap. The heel he touched shifted slightly and fell to one side. That's when the gunman noticed that the boots were still wrapped around Will's feet, which just happened to be sticking out from the bushes.

"What the hell?"

As those words slipped out of the gunman's mouth, he saw a hand reach out from the bushes to slip around the back of his head. It was like something from a kid's nightmare, and struck a chill in the gunman that went right down to the marrow in his bones.

"Your friend is alive," Clint said in a harsh whisper. "If you want to stay the same way, you'll do exactly what I tell you to do."

Although there was plenty of fight in the gunman's eyes, there was also just enough fear to keep it in check.

In a quick, fluid motion, Clint used his free hand to pluck the gun from the other man's holster. "What are you men doing here?"

The gunman glared at Clint and ground his teeth together. His silence came to a quick end when he heard the hammer of his own gun being thumbed back into firing position.

"These are our woods," the gunman replied. "We been living here for months."

"Doing what? Robbing anyone who comes through?"

Smirking, the gunman nodded. "Or just them that fall asleep in the wrong spot."

"So that was you, huh? You and who else?" When he didn't get a response quickly enough, Clint stuck the barrel of the gun he'd taken into its owner's ribs. "You're not nearly sneaky enough. Who else was there?"

"Me and Chris. We could'a killed you where you lay. Could'a slit your throat, but we didn't."

"And I could have shot you and your friend when you still had your dick in your hand, so I guess that evens things up. Why all the shooting if you just mean to rob folks?"

"Jack was coming to Mud Foot to pick up something. It was supposed to give us the right to a whole lot of money that was lost up on Farewell Mountain."

"You mean that train that was supposed to have crashed?"

The gunman nodded.

"I haven't even seen any tracks," Clint said. "What

makes you think that train isn't just some sort of rumor or legend?"

"Jack's sure of it. Said he seen the tracks when they was being built. Most of us ain't been riding with him that long, but a few have. Jack ain't got no reason to lie about something like that."

"So what was Jack supposed to be picking up in town?"

"I don't know. Some sort of claim or deed or some such."

THIRTY-SIX

When Clint made his way back to where he'd left Jeb, he thought that the other man had run off somewhere. When he saw the rifle barrel protruding from some of the surrounding bushes, Clint hoped that things hadn't taken a very bad turn.

Fortunately, Jeb was on the other end of that rifle. He was just a little better at hiding than Clint had thought.

"I . . . I was just about to come after you," Jeb stammered.

"No need for that, but it's good to know you've got me covered."

Jeb took some pride in that, and stepped the rest of the way out of the bushes. "How many were there?"

"Just two."

"Did you . . . ?"

"No, I didn't kill them. You'll just have to remind me to come back and untie them when all of this clears up."

"And . . . what if we don't—"

"Then I'd say those two deserve to sit out there and feed the animals," Clint interrupted. Reaching out to pat Jeb on the shoulder, he added, "We can't think about things like that. We're going to get through this just fine. Don't worry about it."

After taking a deep breath, Jeb nodded.

"Now, where have you been sleeping these last few days?" Clint asked.

"I found a cave at the foot of the mountain. It's not too far down the road from where you're camped."

"All right then. Head back there and wait for me. Is there a way you can mark it so I won't pass it by?"

"I can tie some sticks together that point right to it."

"How about you drive two sticks into the ground and angle them in the right direction? That way I'll know what to look for and you won't attract too much attention from anyone else who goes that way."

"Smart thinking," Jeb said as he tapped his temple. "How long will you be?"

"Shouldn't be long. I'll try to head out first thing in the morning. If I'm not there by late afternoon, that means there's trouble. Well, more trouble."

"I understand."

"Now get going."

Jeb headed back toward the road without looking back. It was plain to see that he was rattled, but he was still getting along pretty well. Clint was actually surprised with how good Jeb was doing under the circumstances. Once the sound of Jeb's footsteps could no longer be heard, Clint followed in the man's path and kept a lookout for anyone that might be following him.

Clint made it back to his own camp without noticing anyone else lurking about in the woods. Since he'd also managed to lose track of where Jeb was, he figured that the other man was sneaking well enough to travel the rest of the way without an escort.

Despite all that had happened, Clint hadn't even been gone for an hour. The sky was just starting to show the first traces of dawn and that light was enough to make it easier for him to move through the dense foliage. His eyes seemed to becoming used to the shadows and the mass of green that used to obscure almost everything from view.

Now, he could pick apart the differences between all the different greens, which made it a whole lot easier to maneuver through the leaves without kicking up a ruckus. Clint was even getting used to the scratches and cuts in his hands, arms, neck, and face that came from getting personal with so many different branches.

After all that he'd done in such a short amount of time, the hardest task was to try and look relaxed when he lay down and stretched out in the spot where he'd been lying before. Clint did his best to slow down his breathing so at least he didn't look as though he'd been crawling and running for the last hour. Once he found a comfortable spot, however, the real test was to keep from falling asleep for real. When he heard the sound of rustling leaves, he kept his eyes shut and his hand fairly close to his Colt.

The rustling was quick and barely noticeable at first, but slowed down once it got closer. Next came footsteps that were almost light enough to be lost under the sound of the breeze. But since Clint had been expecting those sounds, he cracked open his eyes. Sure enough, he spotted Carmen making her way back into the camp.

Her head snapped toward him the moment he got a look at her, and her hand flashed to the gun stuck under her belt.

THIRTY-SEVEN

"Oh, you're awake," Carmen said pleasantly.

Clint sat up and stretched his arms. "It was a busy night."

"You can say that again. I was just about to make some breakfast. You want anything?"

"How about some flapjacks and bacon?"

"I think I can whip something up. Are cold beans and coffee close enough?"

"Sure." As he watched her move around the camp, Clint waited for her to mention where she'd been. By the time the coffee was ready, it became clear that she wasn't going to say a word about it.

"I did have a little trouble sleeping," he said.

As he'd expected, that caused Carmen to twitch a little at the corner of her mouth. It was a reaction that years of poker playing had gotten him used to. Whatever she said next was going to be a bluff.

"Really?" she asked. "I slept like a log."

"I swear that you weren't here when I rolled over one time."

She scooped up the rest of the beans that were on her plate and shrugged. "Maybe it was a dream."

"It was no dream. You were gone."

"Clint, there's no place for me to go. Trust me."

"You know something? I actually believe that you used to live around here. You know the area well enough for that. I also believe a good portion of what you told me about your past. But I know for a fact you left here during the night and then snuck back."

Wiping off her plate and stuffing it in her saddlebag, she asked, "Is it a crime for someone to stretch their legs in the middle of the night? Do I need to tell you about every little thing I do?"

"I can understand if you'd want to hide something form me."

"Hide something? Like what?"

"Like the fact that you were the one who robbed me."

When she heard that, Carmen froze. The expression on her face didn't give anything away, but it was easy enough to see that her mind was moving at a hundred miles an hour.

"What on earth would make you think that?" she asked.

Clint stood up and calmly cleaned off his own plate. He stuck that and his spoon into his saddlebag. "You snuck up on me," he said simply.

After waiting for a moment to see if he was going to say anything else, Carmen let out a little laugh. "What are you talking about?"

"I'm not the sort of man who looks for trouble, but there's always plenty of trouble looking for me. Throughout the years, a man in that position starts to pick up certain habits. He sits with his back to a wall. He looks to see who's got a gun and who doesn't. He notices how a person carries themselves to see how well they can move.

"And he tends to be a light sleeper," Clint added as he locked eyes with Carmen. "It's hard to sneak up on a man like that. I've caught plenty of thieves trying to sneak into my camps, but someone managed to sneak in, clean me out, and sneak away. That's a hell of a feat."

"I still don't see what this has to do with me," Carmen said.

"If I hadn't forced myself to stay awake last night, you would have been able to sneak out of camp without me knowing a damn thing. That's a real talent. You should be proud."

Carmen stood up and stepped forward. Her eyes blazed defiantly and her hands were propped upon her hips. "If you wanted me to leave, all you had to do was ask. I know some men get strange after they have a night like we did, but Jesus Christ!"

"Those gunmen that are out there are the same group who robbed me," Clint continued as he walked around her and crossed over to where Muriel was standing.

"Well, there you go," she said. "People who live in places like this tend to be light on their feet."

He looked at her with mild amusement. "Light on their feet?" he asked. "You mean so you don't rile up any bears or the like?"

She nodded. "These aren't the first robbers to hide out in the woods. Dangerous men live in the mountains."

"Even more dangerous ones are around this one. What I'm trying to figure out is what you intended on doing," Clint said. "I mean, if you wanted to kill me, you could have made a move by now. Lord knows, you'd be able to get behind me if you wanted to."

The expression on Carmen's face shifted from upset to hurt the more Clint spoke along those lines. "I've trusted you this entire time," she said quietly. "After the way you came along and saved me from that ditch when I thought I might be buried there, I thought you were a real hero. And then we had a time like last night, which I've never had with another man."

When she saw Clint give her an even more intent stare, she added, "I mean I've never had a night that good with another man. The point is that I trusted you with my life and in the situation we're in, we're going to need all the trust we can get just to make it out of these woods in one piece."

Clint nodded and said, "I didn't want to think the worst of you, but there was always something that didn't set right with me."

"The type of man who sits with his back to a wall needs to be suspicious. Isn't that right?"

"Fair enough." Crossing his arms, Clint looked her straight in the eyes and said, "All right then, answer two questions and we'll see about regaining some of that trust."

She let out a relieved breath. "I'd like that."

"First of all, when those robbers got hold of you and tried to force themselves upon you, why'd they let you keep that Smith & Wesson?"

"I found it after I got away."

Having expected something like that, Clint nodded and reached out to flip open Carmen's saddlebag. "My second question," he said while removing something that had caught his eye a while ago, "is how did you find my spyglass?"

THIRTY-EIGHT

Carmen's eyes never left the telescope in Clint's hand. First, she tried to look surprised, but didn't try to keep that up for long. Second, she looked guilty, until she finally gave him an angry glare.

"So what are you going to do now?" she asked. "I know better than to try and outdraw you, so you'll just have to shoot me in cold blood if that's what you're after."

"It's not."

"What then?"

"I want you to tell me what you were supposed to do at the end of all this."

She looked around a few times and then asked, "At the end of all what?"

Now, it was Clint's turn to put on the angry glare. "I've got no problem believing that we crossed paths by accident the first time. Hell, I didn't even know where I was going when I was out riding. Even crossing paths the second time was a big coincidence. I can buy that. But don't take me for an idiot by telling me that gaining my trust and everything else that followed was just a strange twist of fate!"

She didn't flinch when Clint raised his voice, even though his tone came as a bit of a shock to himself. Instead, she stood there calmly and waited for him to be done.

"And if you tell me you were going to give this back," Clint said as he held out the telescope, "then you might as well just start running right now."

"You want to know what truly was an accident?"

"Tell me."

"Falling into that ditch was an accident," she said. "I don't care how long you've lived in these parts, there's no way for anyone to know every bump there is." Shaking her head, she walked back to the small clearing and sat down.

Carmen let out a breath that she seemed to have been holding for a good, long while and slid her fingers through her hair. "We didn't know you'd be coming. Jack told us about someone in town who'd traded shots with Abe and Matt, but we didn't know who it was. Even if we did, that wouldn't have mattered.

"We came here all the way from Oregon and I happened to find you when I was out swiping supplies. Remember how surprised I was when I saw you while I was lying in that ditch? That wasn't an act."

"I can believe that," Clint admitted. "But right now, the way you're looking at me with those wide, sad eyes . . . I'd say that might be an act."

She tried to hold onto the expression she was wearing for another few moments before letting it drop completely. It was almost like seeing a statue crack and fall apart just to show something else entirely underneath it.

"So, you're not going to shoot me and you're not going to trust me," she said. "That brings me back around to asking what we're going to do now."

Surprisingly enough, Clint smiled at her. It wasn't a confident smile or even a victorious one. In fact, it was a genuine smile that seemed even odder when compared to the look on Carmen's face. "Is Carmen even your real name?"

Rolling her eyes, she replied, "No."

"What is it?"

"Christine."

Clint nodded. "And everyone else in that gang calls you Chris?"

"Yeah."

"I heard them talking about you a few times."

"Nothing bad, I hope. So, do you want me to leave?"

"Nope," Clint said. "I want you to tell me why you're in this line of work."

"To make money," she said. "And you can keep the speech about doing good and doing bad, because I've already heard it."

"Actually, I would have been disappointed if you'd said anything else. You want to know where we go from here? I say we go straight ahead with where we were going before."

She cocked her head to one side and examined Clint closely. "What's the angle?"

"No angle. I think we can work well together. I also think you'd rather work with someone like me than the men you've been working with up to now."

"Why's that?"

Clint narrowed his eyes and lowered his voice to something similar to a snarl. "Because when things get hotter as far as me and your other friends go, I'm not about to walk away and let them go on harming innocent folks. I think you know that much already."

"You're stubborn as hell," Christine said. "I'll give you that much."

"You got that right. And if your friends aren't ready to walk away when they have the chance, things will get bloody. I'd rather have it any other way, but we both know your friends aren't the type to take defeat too gracefully."

As much as Christine wanted to say otherwise, she knew she wouldn't be able to pull it off with a straight face.

"And I know that you can take your defeats pretty well," she said with a smirk.

"If you're talking about robbing me, I let you get away with that stuff."

"No—you were snoring loud enough to wake the dead."

Waving off the debate rather than stay on a sinking ship, Clint asked, "So would you rather work with me on this or would you prefer to take your chances with the bunch of killers you've been riding with?"

Christine's eyes fixed upon Clint as she studied him carefully. "How do you know those killers aren't like a family to me? Maybe they're closer than brothers after we've been working together for so long?"

"If that was the case, you wouldn't have looked so interested when I brought up the possibility of leaving them."

"A few of them aren't too bad," she said with honesty. "And I wouldn't like to set them up to be killed."

"I'm not the sort to kill a man without giving him the chance to walk away. If I was, this conversation would have been over a hell of a lot sooner."

Clint was still watching every move she made and measuring every breath she took. There was no way for him to know exactly what she was thinking, but he could tell that Christine was most definitely weighing her options.

"What are you asking me to do?" she asked.

"Just steer those friends of yours out of these woods so the folks who live here can do so in peace again. It can happen easily or it can get messy. If any blood is spilled, it will be because one of those gunmen pushed things too far. You can't honestly tell me that something along those lines wouldn't have happened sooner or later."

"There are some hotheads in that group."

"And that's another reason we've been talking for so long," Clint said. "Someone with talents like yours doesn't need to ride with a bunch of assholes who fire their guns just to hear them go off. No matter what you said to me or what lies you might have told, I don't think you're a killer. A hell of a thief," he added with a smile, "but not a killer. My guess is you've been waiting for a chance to break off on your own."

By this time, Christine had stopped trying to put on a front. She could read Clint well enough to know that he could look right through it anyway. "They weren't always like that, you know. We used to rob stagecoaches or a store every now and then to earn some money, but nobody would get hurt. That was back when a man by the name of Bert Langstrom was the boss."

"What's Bert doing now?" Clint asked.

"Not a lot, since Jack shot him three times in the face over a matter of ten dollars." She shook her head and let out a breath. "When you found me in that ditch, part of me was hoping you'd kill them two that walked by us. Those assholes wouldn't have lifted a finger to help me just because I wouldn't let any of them crawl into my pants at one time or another."

"We're already past that. All that's left is to finish what we've already started. All that needs to change is the name I call you."

Christine laughed as if she could hardly believe what was running through her mind. "What's in this for me?"

"You get to have a closer look at this mountain without those others getting in your way. If there's no train, we can part ways quietly and without a fuss and you can have a chance to leave those others behind as well."

"And if there is a train?"

"Then you can split the money three ways."

"You've got a deal."

THIRTY-NINE

The cave smelled like mold and smoke. Despite the gritty haze that hung in the air, Jeb pressed himself against the back wall where the fog was the thickest. Rodents and bugs skittered from one shadow to another, sending the scratch of their steps throughout the cave.

Everything Jeb owned was in that cave with him. It wasn't much more than a small pile of tools and a few bags of supplies, but he was ready to guard it with his life. He kept his gun across his lap and at the ready. His eyes remained glued to the small opening no more than eight feet away.

When he heard the crunch of boots against the leaves he'd spread out, Jeb brought the rifle up to his shoulder and curled his finger around the trigger.

"Jeb?" came the whispered voice. "You in here?"

Lowering the gun, Jeb was so anxious to get to the opening that he almost stood up and cracked his head against the rocky ceiling. "I'm here, Clint! Come on in."

Clint pushed aside some branches and took off his hat to keep from making the same mistake Jeb had almost made a few moments ago. He grumbled to himself as he stepped a few paces into the cave. "I wish you would have told me there were so many caves around here. I think I riled up every bat in this mountain."

"There are other caves?"

"Never mind that. I need you to get moving and work your way up the side of this mountain."

"Where are we going?"

"You're going on your own," Clint explained. "I'll meet you along the way."

That put a definite frown on Jeb's face. "Why split up?"

"Because I've got someone along with me and I'm not sure if I want to show her all my cards just yet."

"Is that the same lady that was in your camp?"

"Yeah, but she's actually one of those robbers."

Jeb tightened his grip on the rifle and took a few reflexive steps back. This time, he knocked his head so hard against the roof of the cave that it took the hat right off his head. "She's one of them?"

"I'm pretty sure she'll work with us rather than against us, but I want to keep you out of harm's way until I'm certain."

"And when will you be certain?"

"Look," Clint said with exasperation creeping into his voice, "there are some trails that lead up this mountain that are pretty well hidden. Do you know the ones I'm talking about?"

"I stuck to the road when I went up, but didn't go too far."

"Well, these trails are a little ways around and wander up the side. At least, they did as far as I can tell. I happened upon them not too long ago and it looked like nobody's been up there for a while. I want you to take those trails up and then work your way around to meet us. Christine and I will be sticking to the road."

"How far away are these trails?" Jeb asked.

Clint scratched a quick map in the dirt, showing Jeb how to find the trails he'd stumbled upon before he'd gotten robbed. When he was done, Clint asked, "Think you can find them?"

Jeb nodded. "If not, I'll just get back onto this road and find you from there."

"Sounds good. If we both move at a regular pace, we should be able to meet up again by tomorrow night. Think you can keep hidden and stay healthy for that long?"

"I may not know about fighting a gang of armed men, but I can make it on my own in the woods."

"Perfect."

"What are we going to do when we meet up again?"

"Trying to stay away from those gunmen should be our top priority."

"What about that train?" Jeb asked. "That's what they're here for, isn't it?"

"Yeah."

"Well, if we could find it first, then maybe we could put them off the trail."

Clint let out an exasperated sigh. "I thought you were after a place to call home. If I knew this was just a hunt for some treasure that probably doesn't even exist, then you can go look for it on your own."

"I'm just saying we could cover up the wreck or hide it so they'll leave."

Stepping forward, Clint put his hands on Jeb's shoulders and looked him straight in the eyes. "Men like these wandering around in this rough country and shooting each other in the back is why this place is called Farewell Mountain. Plain old greed is more than enough to take up the slack for a curse. Don't fall into that trap yourself."

Jeb nodded. "You're right. It's just that it seems awfully tempting."

"So does getting filthy rich off of poker, and look how that turned out."

This time, Jeb looked as if he'd been splashed in the face with cold water. He blinked a few times and said, "You're sure right about that. I'll find my way to those trails and then meet up with you tomorrow night."

"That's the plan," Clint said with a confident nod.

Dropping his voice to a near whisper, Jeb asked, "But what about those men?"

"When I left Christine, we were well ahead of them. The closest group are still tied up a good ways from—"

"No," Jeb interrupted as he stabbed a finger toward the mouth of the cave. "I mean *those* men."

Clint turned to look over his shoulder, and was just in time to see a pair of men wearing bandannas shove their way through the low-hanging branches. Their own rifles were at the ready and their eyes would fall upon Jeb's cave at any moment.

FORTY

The two gunmen moved through the bushes with practiced ease. Either they were more experienced at walking through the woods without stirring up too much noise, or all of the men were getting used to their demanding surroundings.

Although their eyes were taking in everything they could, their steps were taking them almost directly toward the cave. As they got closer, they slowed their steps up even more until they made next to no sound whatsoever.

They were less than ten paces away from the cave when they felt light taps on their shoulders. Spinning around in unison, they almost blasted Christine right out of her boots.

"Jesus, Chris," one of the men grunted. "That's a real good way to get yourself shot."

She kept her hands where the men could see them and grinned. "Just testing your reflexes. You passed. As far as your hearing goes, I can't give you very high marks on that."

"Did you know two of the others were bushwhacked not far from here?" the second gunman asked.

"No. I've been scouting on my own."

"Is that where you've disappeared to?"

She backed away from the men and started walking

away from the cave. "Is that what everyone's so cross about? Last time I checked, it was my job to be the scout around here."

"Scouting's one thing," the first gunman said as he followed her. "Disappearing is another. Jack don't like that."

She tossed a wave over her shoulder and said, "Jack doesn't like much of anything. Besides, I checked in with him last night and he said everything was just fine."

Both of the gunmen laughed at that. Once the initial tension had been broken, they fell into a much easier step behind Christine. Of course, the playful twitch in her hips also had something to do with that.

"If you think everything's just fine," the second man said, "then I know for damn sure you haven't talked to Jack."

"We're headed up this side of the mountain," she recited while pointing vaguely toward the looming mass of rock. "We'll uncover some train wreck, get filthy rich, and all the rest."

Shaking his head, the first gunman let out a strained breath. "Sounds like she's talked to Jack."

Christine turned to face both men wearing a serious expression on her face. "Look, I'll tell you the same thing I told him, which is that I haven't found a damn thing on or around this mountain."

"You sure about that?"

"Where do you think I've been since Joey got shot? I've been up and down these trails and haven't found anything."

The first man nodded. "We're supposed to be looking for the asshole who's got that deed, but we ain't even found any tracks. I mean, there's supposed to be tracks somewhere if there's supposed to be a train, right?"

"Last time I checked," Christine replied. "Does anyone really think that other fellow with the deed is around here?"

"That's what Melvin says."

Spitting out a grunting laugh, the second gunman added, "Melvin's a weasel who'd say anything to save his skin. I'm surprised Jack ain't killed him yet for losing that deed in the first place."

The first gunman looked Christine up and down, while nodding at what he saw. "You coming back with us, Chris?"

"I'll catch up before sundown. If you see Lou, tell him to talk some sense into Jack so we can get the hell out of here. There hasn't been anything worth stealing in these parts for close to a year."

For a moment, neither gunman said a word. The odd part was that they both looked as if they had plenty to say. Finally, after looking at each other for a few seconds, they looked back to Christine.

"We talked to Jack ourselves," the first gunman said. "Lou and Jack haven't exactly been seeing eye to eye."

"They never have."

"No, Chris. It's been worse lately. I don't think Lou's buying what Jack's been selling if you catch my meaning."

She nodded. "Send them my best, huh? But don't let yourselves get run off a cliff either. Do you catch my meaning?"

"Sure do. Take care of yourself."

Nestling their rifles in the crooks of their arms, both gunmen waved to Christine and headed back for the main road. Both of them knew better than to try and catch sight of her after that.

FORTY-ONE

Clint emerged from the cave where he'd been crouching once he saw the coast was clear. Fortunately, Christine had kept the gunmen's backs turned long enough for him to get to one of the other caves he'd found when he'd been searching for Jeb's.

"I thought you were going to be right back," she said as she emerged from the woods as if by magic.

"And I thought you were going to stay put and wait for me."

Christine shrugged. "When you didn't come back right away, I thought something might have happened to you. Did you find a better way for us to go up the mountain?"

"No," Clint replied. "But I almost got caught by those other two. Thanks for steering them away."

"What are partners for?"

They made it back to where the horses were waiting and climbed into their saddles. Now that he had a higher vantage point, Clint took a closer look into the trees where the two gunmen had gone. As far as he could tell, they were nowhere nearby.

"I couldn't help but overhear you talking to those two," Clint said. "Was that true what you told them?"

"Was what true?" she asked.

"About what you said to the one running that gang while you snuck off."

"Oh, Jack? That part was true. Him and Lou don't exactly see eye to eye. That draws a line right through the rest of the boys. Some take to being heavy-handed and quick on the trigger like Jack, while others like to do things the way we used to do it like Lou."

"Sounds like something we can use."

"I already am using it. Weren't you listening?"

She snapped the reins and got her horse moving along the path that went up the mountain. By now, Eclipse pretty much knew not to let the mare get too far ahead.

"So you want to split up those two sections of the gang?" Clint nodded approvingly. "That would make things a whole lot easier."

"And if you had a better idea of where we were headed when looking for this train, or if you could get your hands on that deed, that would go a long way in that same direction."

"I might be able to help with that."

She brought Muriel to a stop and shifted so she was facing Clint, more or less head-on. "We can spar like this all day long to pass the time, but this deal was supposed to be a partnership, remember?"

"And I just recently found out you're a member of the same group that was trying to kill me not too long ago. Remember?"

"I can understand you not trusting me, but we won't get anywhere unless we put a little faith in each other."

Clint pulled in a breath and finally said, "I should be able to get us that deed. At the very least, it'll show us what your boss is after."

"Jack's not my boss, but that's great news. That deed wouldn't be hidden in that cave, would it?"

"No," Clint replied with a laugh. "Not hardly."

"All right then. As long as we're asking questions, how about you tell me what you were doing in that cave?"

"Hiding from your friends. That's about it."

She narrowed her eyes as if she was focusing in on something at the back of Clint's mind.

"I was talking to someone who might be a big help to us," Clint said after a few more seconds of that scrutiny. "But I swear, that deed isn't in that cave and I don't have it anywhere on me. You can search me if you don't believe me."

"I just might do that," she said with a wink.

Now it was Clint's turn to scrutinize her. "You seem awfully cheery."

"Actually, I'm starting to think that we might just be able to pull this off. I mean, someone in my line of work can't be too picky where her partners are concerned, but these boys I've been with are headed for a fall. Now that it looks like I won't have to fall along with them, things are looking better than they have for a while. Kind of makes me glad that I spotted you sleeping like a baby back then."

"By the way," Clint said. "I think you owe me some money."

"What?"

"Just the money that you stole from me when I was sleeping like a baby."

"You'll have to take it from Jack," she said with no small amount of disgust. "He takes more than half of what comes into that gang."

"Let me guess. It didn't used to be like that?

"Not hardly."

"Which is another good reason to get out as soon as you can."

She shrugged and said, "A girl's got to fend for herself the best she can."

"And so does a man," Clint said while holding out a

hand palm up. "Part of that involves not letting someone get away with stealing from him."

"Let's just see if we can make it through this. If both of us are still alive when it's done, we'll see about paying you back."

The ground beneath them was beginning to slant upward and the trees were starting to thin out. Already, Clint could feel his breaths coming a lot easier than when he'd been surrounded on all sides by a wall of green.

"Don't you think you'll be able to split some of the men away from the rest?" Clint asked.

Before Clint had left to look for Jeb's cave, he and Christine had been hashing out a plan that would get both of them what they were after. It was a solid enough plan that Clint had started to lose some of the regrets he'd had about letting Christine know that he knew about her initial deception. Now, however, some of that confidence was showing a bit of rust.

But Christine nodded confidently and looked around at the changing scenery. "Oh, I should be able to cut the numbers down. I'm sure those two I talked to will spread around what I told them to the ones that most need to hear it."

"And that should be enough to whittle down some of the guns we'll be up against?"

"Oh, certainly. Once I get back to them and talk to Lou, I might even be able to cut the number of men we need to worry about in half."

"So that means, around four or five?"

She looked over at Clint as if he'd just started clucking. "That would be nice." After a few more seconds of watching him, her expression changed a bit. "Are you serious?"

"One of the first men I got a hold of told me there were seven members of the gang. I killed one and if you could take away half of what's left, that would only leave—"

"Seven members of the gang? That's what you thought?"

"Sure. Give or take."

"Oh, well, if you're willing to give or take, then that's not so bad." She laughed and said, "Whoever you talked to lied through his teeth."

Clint's eyes narrowed and he felt his stomach clench into a knot. It wasn't often that someone was able to sneak a bluff past him, but he was only human after all. "How many men are there?"

"Closer to seventeen," she said. "Give or take."

FORTY-TWO

When Jeb caught up with Clint, it was early evening and the sun was covering Farewell Mountain with a thick curtain of soft red light. The tops of the trees looked more like a choppy ocean that was all one giant thing rather than thousands of leaves and branches.

Clint was alone and stood alongside the road, waiting quietly with Eclipse's reins in hand. He had no trouble at all picking out the shape that was coming toward him. In fact, he felt that his eyesight had become sharper in the days he'd spent crawling through the bushes.

"It's good to see you," Jeb said. "Hope you weren't waiting long."

"Did anyone spot you?" Clint asked.

"I doubt it. You're the first person I've seen since we parted ways the last time. There were a few rustlings here and there, but none of them made it far up the mountain."

"Did you get a chance to get a look at the land?"

"You mean the land I won? I sure did! It's a nice patch of land on the other side of that far ridge. It looks a lot farther than it is, so I could probably get there in a few hours. Quicker if we ride."

"Didn't you ride a horse here to begin with?"

"I left her on that patch of land. It's easier for me to sneak about that way."

Clint reached down to offer Jeb his hand. "Climb on behind me and show me the way."

"We're just taking the road?"

"We don't have a lot of time. Just climb up and I'll explain as we go."

Jeb got into the saddle behind Clint and told him which way to ride. Once Eclipse got moving at a good pace, Clint finally broke the silence between them.

"Things are a little worse than I thought they were," he said.

Jeb grumbled to himself and asked, "How much worse?"

"We're up against some bigger numbers than I originally thought. The good news is that we should only be going against half the gang that's been giving us all the trouble."

"Half? That's good news, isn't it?"

"That still means we're going to be up against nine or ten men."

"But . . . there's only two of us."

"Yeah. That brings me back around to what I said the first time. Even so, that doesn't mean we can't do this. It might be a little tougher than I thought, since bigger groups tend to be more gun-happy. Also, the men that are left will probably be the worst of the bunch. From what I've heard, they also know this part of the mountain fairly well. At least, one of the men with them will know it pretty well."

"Anyone I know?"

"I think Melvin is working with the leader of the gang. The lady I was riding with has told me that the gang was on its way to pick up that deed just as Melvin was gambling it away."

"That's not a smart thing for Melvin to do," Jeb said.

Clint laughed and replied, "You'd be amazed at how

stupid some men will get when they think they've got a winning hand. Anyway, Melvin's along for the ride, so he must know a good way to get to that land. They're convinced that deed will help them get their hands on that train that was supposed to have wrecked on this mountain. Have you seen anything in that regard?"

Jeb was quiet for a few seconds as he thought it over. Finally, he said, "It's a beautiful patch of land, but there's no train."

"What about any tracks?"

"Nope. None that I could see anyway."

"That might work to our advantage," Clint said. "There's a slim chance that those men will see they're on a wild-goose chase and then just leave."

"Only a slim chance?"

"We've all come a long way, Jeb. Hell, even *I'm* itching for a fight after all this sneaking around. Chances are, those gunmen won't even be listening to a word I say."

"So . . . maybe we shouldn't say anything."

"No matter how anxious I may be, I'm not going to ambush anyone unless that's the only choice I've got."

"Then maybe we should just ride out of here and let those men have the land," Jeb said in a defeated tone of voice. "I can always find somewhere else to make a new start."

Clint shook his head. "We've come this far. There's no reason to see it through. Besides, letting someone get their way just because they're ready to pull a gun out never sat too well with me. Call it a character flaw."

They rode a little further up the mountain and then took a path that branched off to go around it. Now that they were actually on the mountain itself, finding the spot sectioned out in the deed wasn't too difficult.

The land was just as Jed had described it. A flat patch just big enough to hold a house and a small stable, it backed against a rock wall and looked out on miles of dense woodlands.

"Sitting up here," Clint said, "all those trees actually look inviting."

Jeb smiled and nodded. "I told you. This is perfect. It'll take me a while to build my house, but there's plenty of wood. I think I'll just put together a log cabin."

"That sounds nice."

"You think I'll actually get to keep this land?" Jeb asked.

After a few moments of contemplation, Clint was the one to nod. "There's no way for them to get around behind us. From what Christine told me, these men are going to rely on brute force to take what they want. After that, I'd say they'll lose interest."

"This is an awful lot of trouble just to help one man find a patch of land to settle on. I wish I could offer you some kind of payment in return."

"When I come back to see your log cabin, you can buy me a beer."

Jeb stuck out his hand so Clint could shake it. "You got yourself a deal."

FORTY-THREE

"It's not much farther," Jack growled as he lowered his head to avoid getting another faceful of leaves. "Ain't that right, Melvin?"

Melvin rode on a pack mule in the middle of the group. That meant he had four men in front of him, a few along either side, and about ten behind. "Just follow this road," he shouted. "It'll take us right to it."

Jack craned his neck to get a better look. Although he could see further down the path now that they were out of the thickest part of the woods, he couldn't see anything to get excited about. "Is everyone accounted for? Did Hank and Chris make it back?"

"I'm here," Christine said. "I've only been back for a few minutes, so I don't know about Hank."

"Hank's missing," one of the other men said. "Has been for a while."

"We'll find him when we find that train. There'll be plenty of time once we claim that land and get our hands on that deed. After that, there won't be nobody who can take away what we find. Ain't that right, Melvin?"

"Yes," Melvin said with a little bit of hesitance. "That's right."

Coming up alongside Melvin's mule, Christine patted him on the shoulder and said, "We can trust ol' Melvin here, because he knows right where that train is. Isn't that right?"

Although there were a few shouts from the gunmen, Melvin didn't make a sound.

"I mean, you have been there to see it, right?" Christine asked. "You know right where to take us and right where the money's buried. All we need to do is get through whoever is trying to take it and then carry out a fortune!"

Now, Jack was turning in his saddle to get a look at Melvin. The moment he saw the look on the other man's face, he raised his hand to bring the whole bunch to a stop. The men parted, allowing Jack to move through them so he could get to Melvin.

"You told me this was a sure thing," Jack snarled. "You told me you knew the money was there."

"Actually, I said the money had to be there," Melvin said. "That's what I was told when I got the deed."

"Have you been up there to see the land for yourself?"

"Yes."

"And have you seen the train wreck?"

Melvin wasn't able to meet Jack's gaze, which was more than enough of an answer for him.

"Son of a bitch!" Jack shouted. Quickly looking around, Jack bit his tongue and reached out to grab hold of Melvin's shirt. "The deal was for you to lead us to this spot so we could find the train that's supposed to be there. You told me the train was there."

"It's got to be," Melvin whined. "I've walked over every inch of that mountain, but got ran off by the fellow who used to hold this deed. That was the only spot that anyone guarded and he said it was because the train was there. The man was rich!"

By now, Christine was the only one who'd gotten close enough to hear what was being said. Due to the fire in

Jack's eyes, nobody else really wanted to get too close to him. "And he was rich because of the money he pulled up from that wreck?" she asked.

Melvin nodded furiously. "Yes! That's right!"

"He told you that much, did he?"

"Yes! He swore to it!"

"Then why," Christine asked, while pausing to make sure she had an audience, "did he hand that deed over to you?"

"I won it from him," Melvin squeaked.

She nodded and steered her horse away. "Then I guess everything must be on the straight and narrow." As she passed several of the men, she rolled her eyes and shook her head.

Jack could feel the mood among the gang changing. Where they'd been anxious and ready for a fight over the last several days, they were now quiet and uncertain. It seemed as though all of the travel, harsh conditions, and rough terrain had caught up to them within the space of a few seconds.

"I swear," Melvin said. "I wouldn't lie to you! I need this money as much as anyone else. I saw it myself! The land was signed over to me and the man who had it before found at least a few bags of money. He took it and ran after I won the deed."

"He just had more than he could spend, huh?" Christine said from where she'd stopped.

"Shut your mouth, Chris!" Jack shouted. Turning to Melvin, he clenched his teeth together and spoke in a vicious growl. "I been after this money ever since I heard that train really rolled through here. If I find out you led us out here for nothing, I will skin you alive and nail you to one of these fucking trees so you can dry out."

Melvin was on the verge of tears. "The money's there. I swear to Christ, it's there. I've seen the tracks, but the wreck is too far down for one man to get to. We need a team to get it, which is why the previous owner couldn't—"

"Save it," Jack interrupted. "Me and my men didn't wait around in those fucking trees for you just so you could tell us you're not certain what the fuck you're doing. When this is done, I'll either have my money or I'll cut you apart so slow that hell will seem like the Promised Land."

Jack's eyes remained fixed upon Melvin until the smaller man had sweat pouring in rivers down his face. Turning to the rest of the gang, Jack shouted, "Let's take this goddamn mountain and be done with it!"

Melvin was more than happy to drop back and away from Jack as the gang started moving down the road again.

Christine was near the back of the group by now and having whispered conversations with some of the men. One of those men who talked to her while also making sure to keep out of Jack's sight was Lou.

He didn't look happy.

FORTY-FOUR

Clint could hear them coming long before he could see a single horse. The road made several turns as it wound its way up the mountain and from his position, Clint could see most of it. He didn't even need to use the telescope that he'd found in Christine's saddlebag. If it wasn't in plain sight, it was obscured by foliage. Since Clint had the high ground, all of those things should work in his favor.

"Give me the deed, Jeb," Clint said as he stretched his arm toward the man next to him.

Jeb reached into his pocket, but kept his hand out of sight. Looking over to Clint, he asked, "Can't I keep hold of it? This is all I got."

"I know. Things are about to get rough and the safest place for that deed is with me." When he saw that Jeb was still hesitating, Clint added, "If I truly wanted to take it from you, I could have. Don't you think?"

Sighing, Jeb nodded. "I guess. Here," he said while handing over the folded paper. "Just be sure to take real good care of it for me."

"That's the reason for all of this."

"I still can't believe how much trouble you're going through on account of me."

"Because folks deserve a good life wherever they can get it. Wars have been fought for that much, so it's got to mean something."

Jeb's eyes widened as he pointed down the side of the mountain. "And it looks like we're headed for war right now."

Clint was lying on his stomach at the edge of Jeb's patch of land. There was a drop-off steep enough to make the side below it look more like a rough castle wall. When he looked in the direction that Jeb was pointing, Clint could see several horses breaking out from the trees that hung down low over that section of the road.

The first man to emerge was familiar to Clint. Even though he'd pulled down the bandanna that had been covering his face the last time their paths had crossed, Jack's stern eyes still blazed with the same fire. His long, stringy hair still hung down in a tangle on either side of his face, making him look more like a wild animal than a man.

Other riders emerged from the trees as well, but Jack didn't even glance back at them. His eyes were fixed upon the flat spot further along the path. When he saw Clint stand up, Jack drew his rifle from the holster on his saddle and levered in a round.

"There's nothing up here for you men," Clint shouted.

"I'll see that for myself once I'm up there," Jack said as he took up his rifle in one hand and pulled the trigger.

The shot hissed through the air well away from Clint's head. That shot was only the spark, however, and the flurry of shots that followed was the fire.

Clint dropped down and lay flat against the ground. He twisted around to get a look behind him, and saw Jeb keeping back just like he was supposed to.

While lying flat against the ground, Clint could feel the rumble of all those horses running up the trail. It was like listening to a boulder rolling straight toward him, and only a fool would stay put when they were in front of that.

Once the gunshots had tapered off, Clint jumped to his feet and fired off a shot. The horses were just rounding the final bend before they made it to the section of the trail that straightened out and led right to Jeb's land. Clint picked out one of the leaders in the group, who had just taken aim with his own rifle.

Clint worked the lever to his own rifle, brought it up, and squeezed the trigger. The rifle bucked against his shoulder and sent a round through the air that knocked the rider clean out of his saddle. With the rest of the gang still firing and thundering toward him, Clint spun the rifle in a tight circle around his fingers to lever in another round while reaching across to draw his Colt with his free hand.

Lifting the rifle one-handed and firing with any accuracy was no easy thing. Even though Clint had put that Colt together himself, firing it in his left hand wasn't easy either. Fortunately for him, the riders were so hell-bent on getting up the mountain that they rode straight to him no matter how many guns he held.

The Colt and rifle went off at the same time, spewing fire and smoke toward the riders. Both rounds found a target, but it was the rifle that did the most damage. The man at the receiving end of that shot let out a wheezing moan as his heart was blasted in two. The Colt managed to carve a piece out of Jack's side, but did nothing to slow him down.

"We're almost there!" Jack shouted. "We can take these assholes!"

At that moment, Jeb stepped up to stand at Clint's side with his old hunting rifle in hand. He didn't even flinch at the incoming gunshots as he raised the rifle, took aim, and pulled his trigger. The rifle let out a loud roar and hit one of the riders like a kick from a mule.

Even that wasn't enough to keep the gunmen from swarming over their fallen partners to finally make it to the top.

Half-a-dozen gunmen thundered past Clint and Jeb

while laying down enough gunfire to keep both men moving instead of shooting back. Jack rode right up to Clint
and smiled down at him even though he was bleeding from
several places. The other five men fanned out to line up like
a mounted firing squad.

After a few seconds, the rest of the gang came along to
follow Jack and the first riders. Christine was the second
one to be seen in this group, and she looked around without
so much as acknowledging Clint's existence. She, along
with the rest of that second group, did not look half as impressed as Jack as they glanced about and whispered
amongst themselves.

"I got you, asshole. Better drop them guns," Jack
snarled as he held Clint at gunpoint. Without taking his
eyes off Clint, he added, "If that other one so much as
breathes funny, gun him down."

Clint's rifle as well as the Colt hit the ground near his
feet.

FORTY-FIVE

"Take a look around," Clint said. When he held out his arms to motion toward the emptiness surrounding them, all he got was a whole lot of anxious guns pointed in his direction. "There's nothing up here but land."

Although it took a while for Jack to take his eyes off Clint, he eventually did. When that happened, his victorious smile started to tarnish. "This ain't the place," he grumbled. "It can't be."

Lou rode up and shouted, "Let's see that deed."

"Go on and show him," Jeb said.

Clint stepped forward and held out the folded piece of paper. The moment he was close enough to Jack, that paper was snatched from his hand.

Jack's eyes darted over the words printed on that paper as his smile faded even more.

"What's it say?" Lou asked. When he didn't get a reply, he rode up closer so he could read it for himself. After a few seconds, he turned to the group of riders at the back of the line and said, "This is the place, all right. And I don't see a goddamn train or one goddamn track."

"After all this shooting, Lord only knows who else is headed this way," Christine said. "I don't want to fire one more shot just to get this patch of rocky land." With that, she steered her horse to face the road that had brought her there and snapped the reins.

"Where the hell do you think you're going, Chris?" Jack asked. When he saw several others following her, Jack wheeled around so quickly that his horse started to rear. "You men get back here!"

Lou was the last to head for the road that would take him back down. By the looks of it, there were only five men who weren't going with him.

"You can't leave, Lou," Jack said. "This was partly your idea."

"And it didn't pan out," he said. "That's no reason to spill any more blood." His eyes strayed toward Clint and showed the slightest bit of fear. "His or ours."

"You leave now and we're through!" Jack shouted. "If I see your faces again, I'll shoot 'em off yer damn skulls!"

That got a few backhanded waves and some halfhearted insults, but not much else. In a matter of moments, the only ones left on that flat patch of land were Clint, Jeb, Jack, Melvin, and a few of Jack's most loyal gunhands.

As Jack brought his horse back around, he was in a fit of rage. His face was blood-red and the muscles in his jaw were clenched tight. His eyes kept shifting back and forth as if he no longer even knew what he was looking at.

"You can leave too," Clint said. "There's no reason to be here. Just hand over the deed so Jeb can have his land. Surely it's no use to you."

But Jack looked more like a wild dog than a man. When he let out a breath, nobody would have been surprised if steam hissed out from his nostrils. "Fuck the both of you," he growled.

With that, Jack drew the pistol strapped to his side. The men who'd remained only needed to see that much before they took aim and pulled their own triggers.

In the same instant that Jack had gone for his gun, Clint

dropped to one knee and picked up his modified Colt from where it had been dropped. One of the men to Jack's left was the first to get a shot off, but it had been aimed at Clint's head while he was still standing, and now sailed through open air.

Another shot exploded from a nearby gun, but that was too rushed to get close to its mark.

The moment Clint had a solid grip on his pistol, he pointed it as if he was pointing his own finger and then squeezed his trigger. The Colt barked once and sent out a piece of lead that passed by the shot fired by Jack.

Jack's round clipped a little bit of flesh from Clint's ear.

Clint's shot drilled a messy hole through Jack's right eye.

When Jack's horse felt its rider flop over, it reared up and pumped its front legs in the air. That caused another horse nearby to follow suit and dump its rider onto the ground.

Shots were still flying through the air, but most of them were fired out of sheer panic. The rider who'd been thrown tried to get up, but quickly discovered he'd broken his leg. The moment he turned to take a shot at Clint, he was put out of his misery by a round from the modified Colt.

Even Jeb managed to get back to his gun and fire off a round that found its mark. He was so close to his target by the time he fired, that his hunting rifle nearly blasted one of the gunmen in half.

That left two more gunmen, who took a moment to collect themselves so they could aim. Clint had gotten to his feet by then and prepared himself for the worst.

Even though they could see Clint facing them, both gunmen still tested their luck and lifted their guns to fire.

Clint burned them down with two perfectly placed shots.

As the smoke cleared and the thunder rolled down from the mountain, Clint reloaded his Colt and looked over the side.

"What about the rest of them?" Jeb asked.

"They weren't kidding. They're riding off the way they came."

"I guess that just leaves this one," Jeb said as he pointed his rifle at Melvin.

"I'm not armed," Melvin whined.

"Then get on your horse and leave," Clint said.

It was Jeb who added, "And if I see you anywhere near my property, I'll shoot you on sight."

But Melvin was in too big of a hurry to put up a fight. The moment he got onto his mule, he snapped the reins and got it moving.

Soon, the only sound left to hear was the rustle of a breeze through the leaves.

FORTY-SIX

Clint was too tired to go anywhere.

After keeping watch to make sure none of the others were coming back, he and Jeb set up a camp in the middle of that flat patch of land on the side of Farewell Mountain.

"To be honest," Clint said as he stretched out his legs to look up at the stars, "just being in the open makes this the most relaxing night I've had in a while. After this, I know I'm going to the desert."

"The desert?"

"Yeah," Clint said with a wistful smile. "All that open space. Not a tree in sight. Sounds like heaven right about now."

"Will you be taking that lady with you?"

"Who? Christine? She said she wanted to get out of here and I believe her. If she meant to come back, she would have done it by now. Besides, doing that would mean she'd have a whole lot of explaining to do to those men that decided to go along with her plan."

"So she split those men off from the gang?" Jeb asked.

"She planted the seed. By the looks of it, that was an idea on plenty of other men's minds in that gang. The way my luck's been, I'll probably meet up with them again before too long."

Jeb let out a contented breath. "I thank you for all your help, Clint. I've got a nice plot of land to build my cabin. Then again, I might just hire some builders to do the job for me."

"Builders?"

"You could do the same," Jeb added. "That is, once we take a few days to haul up whatever's left in that wreck I found."

Clint sat bolt upright and looked Jeb square in the eyes. The other man wasn't nearly good enough to pull off a bluff that well. "You're serious?"

Jeb nodded and grinned. "Remember those hidden trails you found?"

Watch for

KIRA'S BOUNTY

295th novel in the exciting GUNSMITH series
from Jove

Coming in July!

GIANT ACTION! GIANT ADVENTURE!

THE GUNSMITH

GIANT

GIANT WESTERNS FEATURING THE GUNSMITH

THE GHOST OF BILLY THE KID
0-515-13622-0

**LITTLE SURESHOT AND THE
WILD WEST SHOW**
0-515-13851-7

DEAD WEIGHT
0-515-14028-7

AVAILABLE WHEREVER BOOKS ARE SOLD OR AT
PENGUIN.COM

J799

**Explore the exciting Old West with one
of the men who made it wild!**

**AVAILABLE WHEREVER BOOKS ARE SOLD OR AT
PENGUIN.COM**

(Ad # B112)

GIANT-SIZED ADVENTURE FROM AVENGING ANGEL LONGARM.

LONGARM AND THE UNDERCOVER MOUNTIE

0-515-14017-1

THIS ALL-NEW, GIANT-SIZED ADVENTURE IN THE POPULAR ALL-ACTION SERIES PUTS THE "WILD" BACK IN THE WILD WEST.

U.S. MARSHAL CUSTIS LONG AND ROYAL CANADIAN MOUNTIE SEARGEANT FOSTER HAVE AN EVIL TOWN TO CLEAN UP—WHERE OUTLAWS INDULGE THEIR WICKED WAYS. BUT FIRST, THEY'LL HAVE TO STAY AHEAD OF THE MEANEST VIGILANTE COMMITTEE ANYBODY EVER RAN FROM.